OLD ONE EYE PETE

Stories from Old New Mexico

Loretta Miles Tollefson

While many of the events in these stories are based on the historical record, they are works of fiction, not biography or history. The thoughts, words, and motivations of the historical figures in this book are as much a product of the author's imagination as are the thoughts, words, and motivations of the fictional ones

"Smith" and "Well-Cultivated" originally appeared in *Story Teller Anthology Magazine.* "Decisions" was originally published at Rope&Wire.com. Some of the other stories in this book were previously published in *Moreno Valley Sketches* and *Moreno Valley Sketches II*, although they may have been subsequently revised for this collection.

ISBN-13: 978-0-9983498-3-1

Palo Flechado Press, Eagle Nest, New Mexico

Other Books by Loretta Miles Tollefson

Old New Mexico Fiction
Valley of the Eagles
Not Just Any Man
The Pain and The Sorrow

Other Fiction
The Ticket
The Streets of Seattle

Poetry
But Still My Child
Mary at the Cross, Voices from the New Testament
And Then Moses Was There, Voices from the Old Testament

A Note about Spanish Terms

Most of the stories in this collection are set in northern New Mexico and reflect as much as possible the local dialect at that time. Even today, Northern New Mexico Spanish is a unique combination of late 1500s Spanish, indigenous words from the First Peoples of the region and of Mexico, and terms that filtered in with the French and American trappers and traders. I've tried to represent the resulting mixture as faithfully as possible. My primary source of information was Rubén Cobos' excellent work, *A Dictionary of New Mexico and Southern Colorado Spanish* (University of New Mexico Press, 2003). Any errors in spelling, usage, or translation are solely my responsibility.

Table of Contents

SPANISH ENCOUNTER

Even in the cooler mountain air, the battered metal helmet and breastplate produced so much heat that the sweat poured off his skin, but seventeen-year-old Elizio de Vaca rode proudly in the center of Don Juan de Ulibarri's two score mounted force, a hundred or more Native allies behind them. The small band of Picuris Pueblans who had fled to the eastern plains would be taught a lesson they wouldn't forget.

Ulibarri and his Spaniards had ridden north from La Villa Real de la Santa Fe to the village of Don Fernando de Taos, collecting allies along the way, then turned east to climb a long narrow valley, then a steep mountain slope. Elizio had expected more mountains, but instead they descended into a valley far longer than its width, the Spanish line strung out across its long green meadows. What a wondrous place it was, Elizio thought, as he turned to look both north and south: surrounded by rich timber, small sparkling streams meandering through its long grasses. On a ridge to his left, elk raised their heads to examine the men in the strange metal garments, then returned to their grazing.

At the head of the column, Ulibarri reined in. The column eased toward him. "We will camp here this night!"

he called to his men. He looked around uneasily. "We are not the first who have stopped here!" he said sharply. "We will post watches!"

~ ~ ~ ~

Elizio was assigned the third watch, that time in the night when the darkness begins to lighten to dawn.

The sun came differently to this mountain valley than it did on the plains, he noted. Its light cast a glow onto the western peaks even while the eastern slopes still lay in shadow. If you didn't know better, you would think the sun was rising in the west. He shook his head and blinked his eyes, allowing them to adjust.

A mist had risen from the streams meandering along the valley floor, creating mysterious shapes and shrouding the long grasses. Elizio squinted. A figure rose from the mist and came toward him. An Apache warrior. Hands shaking, Elizio lifted his spear. Another figure emerged, then another. Elizio opened his mouth to call for help, but the first man's hands were empty, palms up to show he had no weapons. The others also.

"Peace," one of them said. "We would speak to el capitán."

Elizio lowered his spear and thrust out a hand, palm toward the warriors. He forced his voice calm. "You wait here," he ordered. "I will go for him."

~ ~ ~ ~

El sargento mayor Don Juan de Ulibarri strode through the Spanish camp in full regalia, helmet and breastplate gleaming in the mountain sunlight. He stopped abruptly beside the fire where Elizio and his compadres were crouched. They sprang to their feet.

Ulibarri gestured impatiently for them to relax. "The Apaches wish peace," he said. He nodded to Elizio. "You did well to come for me." His eyes swept the other men. "He kept them from the camp until I was informed," he said. "Even with those who seek peace, it is well to be cautious." He nodded abruptly to Elizio and swept on.

"It is an honor," Elizio's friend Tomás murmured behind him.

Elizio turned. "I told them to stay because I was afraid," he said guiltily. "I thought they might capture me if they came farther. I didn't know they truly meant peace."

Tomás chuckled. "You think like el sargento mayor," he said.

Elizio stared down the path that Ulibarri had taken toward his tent. "I was afraid," he said again.[1]

---

[1] In New Spain's northern province of nuevomexico in the Summer of 1706, the Pecos District's sargento mayor , Don Juan de Ulibarri led forty mounted soldiers and at least a hundred Pueblan allies onto the eastern plains. Ulibarri's goal was to retrieve a band of Picuris Pueblo Indians who'd fled Spanish rule. His forces moved north from Santa Fe to Taos, then into the Sangre de Cristo mountains, across the Moreno Valley, and through the Cimarron mountains to the plains. They reportedly met and interacted with a group of friendly Apaches before they reached their destination. This story sets that meeting in the southern end of the Moreno Valley, near today's Angel Fire, New Mexico.

OLD BILL

Old Bill and the two mules had been stumbling south, half-blinded by snow, for three days. When he came over the top of the rise and looked into the valley below, he passed his hand over his face. He must be hallucinating.

He looked again. Sure enough, that was a valley below. The snow was thinner there. A herd of elk had worked large patches clear. Where the snow still held, it was softening quickly. The wolves patrolling beyond the herd were breaking through the crust, snow almost to their hocks.

He studied the layout. Elk, snow melt for water. Bound to be Injuns. He passed his hand over his face again, warming his eyes, and looked again. Sure enough, wisps of smoke rose from the base of the hills at the valley's southern end.

He was coming in peace with little more than the mules and what he was wearin'. They'd feed him, sure. Had probably already seen him. "C'mon, you mules," he said.

~ ~ ~ ~

He entered the Ute camp warily, one hand on the mules' lead rope, his rifle in the other. A man rose and came forward. Old Bill snorted a laugh. "Three Hands!" he said. "I done found you!"

The man studied him. "You searched for me?"

"Well, not exactly. But I sure am glad to find you."

Three Hands nodded. "You are cold."

"Warmer now than I was," Old Bill said. "This is quite a little valley you have here."

"Not so little." Three Hands gestured to the south. "More below."

"Sure am glad I stumbled in," Old Bill said. "I was nigh to freezin' comin' over Bobcat Pass."

The other man looked at the mules. "You trap?"

"I was, but the beavers are iced in nasty hard this winter. Can't get at 'em."

"The signs say the cold will continue."

"That how come you're here?"

Three Hands smiled noncommittally.

~ ~ ~ ~

At dusk, Old Bill wrapped himself in a buffalo robe and lay quiet against the wall of the Ute lodge. This weren't no hunting party, if he savvied correct. They were laying in wait for somethin' and it weren't other Injuns, to his thinking. He wasn't exactly a captive, but Three Hands had made it clear he should stay in camp.

He'd been wandering these parts long enough to have picked up a smattering of Ute lingo. What he'd overheard made him think there were Mexican soldiers headed this way. From Taos, maybe, though it was a hellaciously fool time of year to be coming from that direction.

He studied his situation. He didn't blame the Utes for their plans. It was their country, after all. Theirs and the

Taos Injuns. But he didn't want to be caught in the middle of it neither. He eased out of the robe.

~ ~ ~ ~

Well, he'd got himself away from the Ute war party, but with only his rifle, one beaver trap, and the clothes on his back. As he headed west into the foothills, Old Bill considered his situation. He was moving into the snow, not away from it, and the cold was devilish fierce. The wind howled into his face, bringing dampness with it. No one but a fool would head into this storm, toward the western peaks, instead of down slope. He hoped the Utes would think so, anyways.

He gripped his rifle, resettled the trap looped over his shoulder, and lowered his head, battered hat tilted against the wind. And he'd thought he'd been cold before he entered that valley. He began to climb steadily, careful to conserve his energy, his long legs eating the mountainside.

When he finally stopped to rest, he could see nothing below but blowing whiteness.

~ ~ ~ ~

"Señor, you are still unwell." The young man assisted the older one back to the fireside chair.

"Don't know what I would of done if you hadn't found me."

The younger man shrugged. "Any good Christian would have done the same."

"Ain't many good Christians in this world, then. You feedin' me and all."

A young woman materialized behind them and spoke to the young man in Spanish. He smiled. "She says you do not eat enough to maintain a grasshopper."

"Soon as I get my strength back, I'll be out of your hair."

"Where will you go, if I may ask?"

"Back to the valley."

"The valley you spoke of?"

"Aye. It's a righteous beauty and worth the trouble, I'm thinkin'. There's beaver somewheres there about or I'm a bobcat."

The younger man stared at him quizzically.

"You're thinking I'm still out of my head."

"Oh no, señor."

Old Bill laughed. "Oh yes, señor!" he chuckled.

~ ~ ~ ~

He had found it.

Old Bill stood on the rocky mountain ridge, hat in hand, and peered into the long green valley below. This was the larger section Three Hands had spoken of, sure as shootin'. Meandering streams glinted in the autumn light and the clouds overhead betokened more rain.

Old Bill laughed aloud, replaced his hat, and scrambled down from the rocks. His credit-bought beaver traps rattled slightly as the new mule followed him gingerly down the mountainside. There'd be beaver here, he could feel it in his bones. If not in the valley itself, then surely in the streams flowing from it into the mountains to the east.

"C'mon mule," he said. "We're gonna recuperate my losses and make us our fortune. All we gotta do is stay out of the way of the Injuns and the Mexicans chasing 'em." He chuckled. "Not to mention catamount and bear."[2]

---

[2] The North Carolina-born mountain man William Sherley 'Old Bill' Williams was based out of Taos from the mid 1820s until his death in early 1849. He preferred to trap alone or with a single camp keeper. This was unusual for trappers at the time, but it enabled him to keep his hunting grounds secret. This story assumes that the Moreno Valley and its surrounding waterways was one of these secret places.

Mexico won independence from Spain in 1821. The area north and east of Taos, including the Moreno Valley, which lies between the Sangre de Cristo and Cimarron mountain ranges, was part of their frontier. Williams knew several Native languages and had friends among the Utes, one of the tribes that hunted in the valley. The Ute camp he stumbles upon is located in the upper Moreno Valley, in the vicinity of what would become Elizabethtown, New Mexico.

THAT DAMN MULE

The new mule has already objected to the steep switchback trail of dirt and fist-size rock. This next section is really going to flatten her ears. Old Pete looks back at her, then leans forward and studies the path ahead as he absently pats the more experienced Hepzibah's gray shoulder.

A narrow rain-slicked shelf of fragment-covered black shale juts out of the mountainside over a precipitous drop and a tree-obscured ravine below. Old Pete grunts and glances to his right. A wall of granite and shale frowns back at him. He grimaces. The trail is narrow here and the section behind long and twisted. He has no choice but to move forward.

He slips off Hepzibah, works his way back to Sandy, and strokes her light brown neck consolingly. "We're almost out o' this," he says. "Just hang on a mite longer and then we'll be back on real dirt."

Well, not entirely dirt. But at least it won't be slick wet shale. Sandy jerks her muzzle at him and Pete chuckles. "Just a mite longer," he says again, as much to himself as the mule. He circles her, checking her pack load of supplies and beaver plews, then tightens the knot on her halter rope and maneuvers back to Hepzibah, playing out the rope as he goes.

He stands between the gray mule and the wall of rock and studies the ledge of shale. It's as wet now as it was ten minutes ago. Better not try riding across. Even Hepzibah's likely to object to crossing this with a man on her back. Old Pete shrugs and begins looping the end of Sandy's lead rope around the older mule's saddle horn. It's not an ideal arrangement, but he can't very well lead both animals at the same time. Hepzibah turns her head and nods at him.

Pete chuckles. "You just know what I'm thinkin', don't you?" he asks.

The mule twitches her gray ears, nickers, then turns her head to peer at the ledge. She snorts disparagingly.

"I know, I know," Old Pete says. "Don't you go naggin' me, too. That Sandy's bad enough."

He studies the looped rope, then thinks better of it and ties it properly with a bowlin[3] knot, just in case he needs to release it in a hurry. Then he touches the knife at his waist, confirming it's there, and makes sure his rifle is well seated in the scabbard lashed to Hepzibah's saddle.

He lifts the bridle reins over her head and holds them loosely as he steps out onto the ledge. The mule pulls back slightly, as if questioning his judgment, but when Pete clicks his tongue at her, she twitches her ears and steps gingerly onto the rock.

"Good girl," Old Pete says. "At least one of you's got some sense."

---

[3] The bowlin, also spelled 'bowline', is an ancient knot originally invented to facilitate tying ships to mooring posts. It's easy to tie and untie if it hasn't been pulled too tightly.

They're a quarter of the way across when Sandy's hooves click onto the wet shale. She balks and Hepzibah jerks to a stop. The bridle reins slide across Pete's palm and he tightens his grip on them and half turns, painfully aware of the slick rock underfoot.

Sandy yanks backward and Hepzibah's metal shoes scrape the shelf as she braces against the younger mule's panic. Small pieces of shale skitter toward the drop.

"Take it easy now," Old Pete says soothingly. He steps back, positioning himself between the granite wall and the mule, and tugs on the reins, trying to angle her straight again. But Sandy's lead rope is pulling hard on Hepzibah's saddle horn, and the gray's head twists toward the drop.

Hepzibah's chest strains toward Old Pete and Sandy brays furiously. Her shoes ring against the rock as she tries to scramble to the perceived safety of the dirt track behind her.

"God damn it to hell!" Old Pete growls. He forces his voice calm. "Just take it easy now."

Neither mule responds. He stretches a soothing hand toward Hepzibah's neck. Her ears flick toward him, then toward the ravine. The rope is stretched tight. Sandy takes another step back, and Hepzibah's chest and front hooves are forced closer to the edge.

There's no help for it. He'll have to free the pack mule and hope for the best. Pete reaches to release the bowlin knot.

But just as his fingers touch rope, the younger mule yanks on it again, and twists Hepzibah further toward the ravine. The knot slides out of Old Pete's grasp.

Hepzibah's shoes grate on the shale as she tries both to gain purchase on the rock and to reduce the rope's pressure. Her eyes are wild now, her breath huffing in fear.

Pete lunges, trying again for the knot, and grabs at Hepzibah's saddle with both hands. His feet slip on the wet shale, pulling him off balance, and he lurches into the mule's shoulder, pushing her sideways.

Hepzibah's front hooves scrape frantically and her shoes leave long pale grooves in the black rock as she and Old Pete slide toward the brink. Then man and mule are tumbling together, she braying in terror, he fighting to throw himself out of her way. Above them, Sandy hauls back on the rope, then screams in fury as she too is yanked over the side of the cliff.

Rock. Trees. Dirt. Mule. Pete forces his elbows to his sides and twists, trying to stay out of the way of his animals and their metal-clad hooves. Their legs flail wildly as they tumble. A tree branch whips across Pete's face as he arches around its trunk.

Finally, a sprawling half-dead juniper breaks his fall. Pete gasps, trying to get his breath. He wipes at the blood on his face, then grapples with the tree's broken branches and struggles into a sitting position. The old wood is thick with wet dust and reeks with the urine stench of the tree's crushed gray-green needles. Pete grabs a spiky branch, pulls himself awkwardly to his feet, and stares in horror at the far side of the ancient tree.

Hepzibah has landed chest first, impaling herself on one of the juniper's multiple trunks. Her eyes glaze as Pete watches. Gray mule, dead wood, and living branches are splattered with blood. Pete looks down at his hands and realizes that at least some of the red stickiness he's wiped from his face is the mule's, not his own.

He touches his waist, reflexively confirming that he still has his knife, as his eyes move from the mule's gory chest to the saddle on her back. Sandy's lead rope is still attached to it. In fact, the knot on the saddle horn has tightened. The rope stretches like a freshly-strung bowstring across the bloody juniper and past Old Pete to the top of a craggy piece of sandstone on his right. From there, it cuts a narrow furrow across a rock-studded ridge of dirt that juts down the slope.

Pete can't see Sandy, but he can hear a wheezing sound from the opposite side of the ridge. He struggles out of the juniper's clutches and pitches himself toward the noise. His feet slip on wet rock and debris and send pieces tumbling into the ravine below. He reaches to steady himself on the rope, then thinks better of it.

When he peers over the stony ridge, he's glad he's kept his hands to himself. The mule lies on her side, feet toward the ravine, head pointing away from him. He can just see the rope, which is looped three times around her head and neck, clamping her muzzle shut and wedging up against her windpipe. The battered pack of furs and supplies is still on her back. She wheezes anxiously and her belly shivers, making the pack tremble.

Pete shakes his head. It's a wonder she can breathe at all. He clambers over the ridge, then works up the slope to come in above her, out of reach of her hooves. Sandy's ears flick when she realizes he's there, but she's already discovered the futility of trying to move her head. She snorts and rolls her eyes at him instead.

"There now," Old Pete says. "You did good. You just lay quiet there and I'll deal with that rope. Yessir, you did good." He kneels on the damp slope above her head and strokes her tan muzzle with his left hand as he pulls out his knife with his right. "Now you just lay still, and I'll cut this old rope and you can ease on up nice and slow," he says soothingly. "Real nice and slow now, you hear?"

He leans forward, settles his left hand firmly on the mule's forehead, slips the knife flat between the rope and her muzzle, twists it, and slices swiftly upward. Sandy twitches her ears and snorts at him, but she doesn't try to move.

"That's the way," Pete says. "You just take it real slow now." He slips the knife back into its sheath, then reaches around her head and begins to gingerly unwind the rope.

When he lifts his hands away, Sandy wheezes and staggers to her feet. She braces herself on the slope and shakes vigorously. The pack slews sideways over her right shoulder. She shakes again and it teeters precariously. Her belly expands and contracts as she sucks in loud mouthfuls of air. Then suddenly, she goes quiet.

Pete's eyes narrow. What now?

Sandy peers over her shoulder toward the rocky ridge. Her nostrils flare and she snorts anxiously. She maneuvers around to face the ridge, then snorts again and steps back, away from Old Pete and the rib of rock and dirt behind him.

"I'm afraid that's Hepzibah you're smellin," Pete tells her. He maneuvers across the slope, reaches for the section of rope still hanging from her halter, and strokes her tan shoulder. "Just settle on down now," he says.

But the mule's not interested in settling. Her eyes roll. She snorts impatiently and tries to back farther away from the ridge.

"I know it ain't a good smell," Old Pete says apologetically. "But I can't just leave her there. I've at least got to figure out how to get that saddle and gear off of her." He reaches to scratch the mule's forehead. "You're gonna have to settle on down now, so I can go tend t' her."

Sandy huffs impatiently, her ears almost flat against her neck. Suddenly, her muzzle jerks up, then back, and pulls Pete's feet out from underneath him. He falls onto his rear end, drops the rope, and begins sliding down the damp slope. Only the surface of the soil is wet. His sliding feet tear into the dry rocks underneath, and rocks and dirt rain into the ravine below as Sandy backs further away.

Pete makes a grab for the trunk of a small pine and stops his slide. "All right, if that's how you want it," he grumbles. The pine's needles are still coated with raindrops. He pushes himself to his feet and waves a wet hand at the mule, then the trees below. "Just go on down there a ways and find yourself some place to calm down a mite. I'll be down directly I deal with Hepzibah, poor thing."

Sandy snorts contemptuously and moves down the slope, her hooves sending more dirt and rock into the ravine.

Pete shakes his head, swipes at his face with his wet hands, and begins making his way back to the ridge. "Hell and damnation!" he mutters. "The only mule I've got left is the one that got me in this mess in the first place. Idiot animal. Though I reckon it couldn't get any worse than it is, 'less both of 'em were dead." He scowls. "And there's no tellin' where my rifle is. Sure as shootin' it ain't still in that scabbard."

He lunges onto the near side of the rib of gravel and dirt between him and the old juniper. "Damn that mule!" he grumbles.

Then he reaches the top and stops abruptly. "I'll be damned," he mutters. "No wonder she was in such an all-fired hurry."

A cinnamon-colored bear rears up from the far side of the juniper, its paws and muzzle black with Hepzibah's blood. The beast looks around blankly, as if puzzled by something. Pete drops sharply and rolls out of sight behind the ridge.

But it's too late. The bear has picked up his scent and Pete's drop has sent a noisy scatter of gravel down the slope. More rocks tumble as the bruin comes to investigate.

The creature may be brown, but it's a black bear, not a grizzly. It'll chase anything that moves, even up a tree. There's no point in trying to run. Pete flattens his back and legs against the damp slope, swipes his hands dry on his breeches, and reaches for his knife.

The bear's head and shoulders appear at the top of the ridge. Pete can smell its hot rancorous breath. Its bloody muzzle swings, investigating. As far as it's concerned, the man here and the dead mule behind are all part of the same carrion. The blood smells the same.

Pete grips his knife hilt in both hands and braces it against his chest, point straight up.

As the bear extends an investigating paw, there's an unearthly scream from the ravine below. It doesn't really register with Pete. He has other things on his mind. He bellows a challenge and slashes at the bear's paw.

The blow misses its mark. The bear snuffs at him again, then rears back, gathers itself, and pounces off the ridge, straddling Pete's chest and pinning his upper arms to his sides.

The oily bruin smell is overwhelming. Pete holds his breath and tightens his grip on the knife. His upward thrust is hampered by the bear's weight on his biceps, but he tries anyway, aiming for the chest. The beast only grunts and shifts a little, positioning itself for the kill.

As the dirty yellow claw lifts from Pete's right arm, the scream comes again. It's closer this time, more deadly in intent, and mingled with a mule's terrified bray. But the bear's shift has given Pete more freedom of movement. He shoves upward awkwardly, aiming as best he can for the heart. But again the beast shifts. The blade does nothing but nick its thick pelt.

Something moves on the slope to Pete's left. Old Pete and the bear both glance sideways. Sandy, blood on her flank and braying in terror, tears across the slope. The pack on her back is split wide open now, and cooking equipment and beaver pelts scatter behind her and down the slope.

Then the bear's left paw crashes into the right side of Pete's face. Five blades of excruciating pain. Blood flooding his nostrils and eyes. Pete swallows the metallic taste desperately, fighting the suffocation, the blackness, and the roaring in his head, trying to sense whether his hands still clutch the knife. Just one more try. Just one more chance to give this bastard a taste of its own medicine.

But then the scream tears the air again and the bear lifts away and is gone. Blood surges through Pete's nostrils, choking off his breath, but when he tries to gulp it away, the slight movement in his throat triggers excruciating pain. The wet rocky slope beneath him tilts wildly away from the mountainside, then a roaring blackness overwhelms him.

After a long while, the blackness dims slightly. As Pete comes to, he's aware of flies buzzing around his head and the rustle of wings settling in a nearby tree. The ground under his breeches and shirt is rain damp, but the moisture under his skull is far thicker than mere water.

Somewhere to his left, a slurry of rock clatters down the slope. Pete's heart jerks in panic but his limbs don't respond as they should. When he tries to turn his head, pain sears through his skull.

It's worst on the right. He forces his hand to his face. Loose skin where his right eye should be. Wet slickness of blood. And pain beyond belief or description.

He fights back the nausea that burns in his throat, then gingerly touches his left cheek. There's blood there to, but the flesh is still firm. He cautiously squints that eye open. A buzzard studies him greedily from the top of a nearby ponderosa.

Then the pain cuts through Pete's skull again and the black waves crash over him.

The slope is in shadows when he once again becomes aware of the slant of dirt and rock under his back and legs. The ground is dry now. Even the blood beneath his head has drained off.

A raven caws from the treetops. To Pete's left, there's a shuffling sound, then the huff of expelled breath. For one terrible moment, he thinks the bear has returned. Then a leathery nostril tentatively touches his left cheek.

Pete cautiously squints his left eye open as a mule's chin whiskers brush across his forehead. A chuckle rises in his throat, then pain ricochets through his skull and cuts off his amusement.

Sandy blows softly into his face. The heat of her breath ratchets the pain higher and nausea clutches him again. Pete raises his hand and feebly waves her away.

The mule steps back, but she doesn't leave. Pete takes a deep breath and heaves himself into a sitting position. A red-hot knife jabs his skull and his stomach heaves. He makes a mighty effort, forces the bile down, then opens his mouth slightly, just enough to take in the cool mountain air without triggering another, higher, surge of the pain.

Then he waits, trying to breathe shallowly, forcing himself to stay awake, letting a shaky strength seep into his limbs.

When the sun begins to set and shadows creep across the slope toward him, Pete knows he's out of time. He mutters,

"Alrighty now," and heaves himself upward. Rock and dirt slip under his feet, sending rivulets toward the ravine. The effort to stand throbs through his skull and he staggers drunkenly against it.

Then Sandy limps toward him. Her neck is bloodstained and a hunk of pink flesh hangs loosely from her rump. What's left of the pack dangles precariously beneath her belly. She noses Old Pete's shoulder. This time, he doesn't wave her away.

~ ~ ~ ~

"Damn mule," Old Pete mutters as the curandera places yet another poultice on the right side of his face. "Lost me my outfit, my rifle, and my eye."

The woman pulls back and gives him an impatient look, then says something in Spanish to the American man who's sitting next to the adobe fireplace in the opposite corner, smoking a pipe.

The man takes the pipe from his mouth. "Coulda been worse."

"Hunh," Pete grunts. The curandera's plaster is beginning to work. He tightens his muscles against the prickling, then breathes out. "Could of been better."

The woman moves to the roughhewn table in the far corner of the room and goes back to crushing herbs in her black stone bowl.

Pete slews his eyes toward the man who found him three days before, clinging deliriously to Sandy's neck beside the rough track to Taos. "That mountain lion gave that damn mule one helluva mauling," Pete says. He moves his head slightly, trying to see past the poultice, then gives up and closes his good eye. "From what little I could see of her, that is," he adds. "She gonna make it all right?"

Ute Park Encounter

Old Bill Williams and Gerald moved steadily down the icy Cimarron River, trapping as they went, a day or two in each location, setting traps, pulling in beaver, skinning carcasses, and stretching plews.

They ate what they trapped until the aroma of fatty flesh drifting from the fire began to turn Gerald's stomach. So when they broke into the small snow-drifted valley Williams called Ute Park, it was more than the scenic beauty that lifted Gerald's heart. A group of perhaps thirty elk browsed on the thick brown grass at the base of a small rocky cliff to the left.

Williams halted, studying the herd. Although the elk seemed unaware of the men and mules, they also seemed restless. Suddenly, a large cow bolted away from the others and across the valley toward the river, on the men's right. As the other elk followed, the source of their anxiety became clear. Three wolves, two small grays and a big black, circled into sight, tagging the stragglers.

The elk surged across the snow and grass, barreled into the stream, then scrambled up the icy bank and into the trees. A young bull, its left hind leg dragging, balked at the river's edge, perhaps wishing for a more shallow ford. The wolves moved swiftly in. As they cut the elk away from the stream, a raven cawed overhead.

Old Bill chuckled, dropped his mule's lead rope, and lifted his rifle. As its muzzle roared, an identical blast echoed from the base of the stone outcropping. The bull stumbled and went down. The wolves darted in, then pulled back. The big black looked over his shoulder, toward the cliff.

Williams' head swiveled, following the wolf's gaze. "Well, I'll be hornswoggled," he said.

An Indian man, his hair in the long braids and high pompadour characteristic of Ute warriors, moved from the base of the rocks. He waved an arm at the wolves, who slunk, tails between their legs, toward the leafless willow brush that crowded the river bank a half-dozen yards downstream. Then they turned and crouched on the grass, their eyes flicking between the approaching man and the dead elk.

"Waagh!" Old Bill groaned. "That Ute's gonna claim that bull, and now him and those wolves have that whole herd most righteously spooked. We don't have a chance in hell of getting another one, and all we've got for supper is that quarter beaver that's on the edge of sour, and that little bit of a tail."

"It may have been your shot that brought that bull down," Gerald pointed out.

"Don't matter," Williams said. His eyes raked the valley. "That Ute does appear to be alone," he added thoughtfully. Then he shrugged. "Well, it's worth a try anyhow. We're two against one."

He grabbed his mule's lead rope and moved forward, Gerald and his mule slightly behind.

The Indian looked up as they moved down the valley toward him, then raised his knife and sliced deep into the elk's belly. He yanked out a long handful of glistening intestine and turned to toss it toward the wolves. The black darted out, mouthed the food, and dragged it off, his companions following obsequiously.

"That's us," Old Bill said over his shoulder. "Those grays."

Gerald grinned and nodded, his eyes on the Indian man, who'd pulled off his buckskin shirt. His bare brown chest rippled in the winter sunlight as he worked on the elk carcass and ostentatiously ignored the two trappers.

Gerald and Williams were within perhaps ten feet before the Ute looked up again.

Old Bill signed "Hello" and the other man nodded noncommittally. His knife sliced systematically into the elk, cutting up the inside of each leg to the hoof.

"That there was a good shot," Williams said, then repeated himself with a few fluent hand signs.

A smile flashed across the Indian's face. "You shot wide," he said in English.

Williams chuckled. He looked down at the carcass and gestured toward its front quarters. "Mind if I just turn him a mite?"

The Indian, who was now incising careful circles around the far back hoof, nodded and paused in his work. Old Bill moved forward, grasped the bull's neck in both hands, and lifted, twisting the body first one way, then the other.

"There's a bullet in each shoulder," he said.

The Ute grinned. "I arrived first. Made first cut."

"You did at that," Williams agreed. "But that's a whole lot of elk for one man to feed on."

The other man's eyes flashed and the knife in his hand lifted slightly. Gerald shifted his rifle, but the Ute's gaze remained on Old Bill. He gestured toward the rocky outcropping and the mouth of the narrow valley that stretched farther north. "My family waits," he said.

"I don't suppose we could trade you a bit of beaver for a haunch?" Gerald asked.

Williams nodded at Gerald. "Beaver fat would be just the thing to flavor that elk," he said. He turned to the Ute. "You know how dry and tough elk can be. Especially this time of year, when the little grass they've had is all dried out and worthless."

The Indian's gaze moved across the valley's patches of still-thick brown grass, then to Williams' face.

"We've got a real hunger for beaver," the trapper continued. "My partner here likes it so well he just truly can't get enough of it. So you could say he's making a sacrifice, offering you some. We can spare you some tail, too, for that matter." He turned to Gerald. "If that's all right with you."

Gerald nodded and Old Bill looked at the Ute. "We just thought we'd do you a favor, is all. Give you something to sweeten the pot and put some taste in that rangy old winter elk."

The man's eyes moved from Williams to Gerald. "Show it me."

Gerald fumbled with the leather thongs that secured the wrapped portion of beaver to his mule's packsaddle and lifted the meat down. "It was fresh yesterday morning," he said.

The Indian leaned forward slightly, his nostrils flaring. Then he pulled back, nodded, and gestured toward the elk carcass. "I trade front left shank," he said. He grinned at Williams. "Your piece."[4]

---

[4] This story is a revised extract from the novel *Not Just Any Man*. Ute Park is a small valley on the Cimarron River about twelve miles downstream from where the river heads in the Moreno Valley, between the Cimarron mountains and the Sangre de Cristo range. Ute Creek flows into Ute Park from the north. The valley is believed to have been a traditional camping and hunting site for the Moache band of Utes. It is still a winter feeding ground for herds of elk.

WATER OF LIFE

"Now what're you gettin' yourself all fired up for?" the matted-haired trapper demanded. "I'm your pa and I can do I want." He lifted the pottery jug from the wooden table with both hands. "I been feelin' a mite poorly since I come in from the mountains and this here's a right good anti-fogmatic."

"Aguardiente," the girl said contemptuously. "Your so-called water of life." She pushed her long black hair away from her face. "Water of hell!"

"Ah, now girlie." He grasped the jug's narrow neck with one hand and reached for her arm with the other.

She slapped at him. "I'm not your girlie any longer. Don't you touch me!"

His eyes narrowed. "I'm still your pappy," he said. "Just 'cuz I been gone five months don't mean you can be disrespectin' me."

She sniffed and turned away.

He gulped down a swig of the liquor. "Where's your ma, anyways?"

"She went to the merchant's to settle her bill."

"Don't want me to know how much she spent while I was gone, huh? What new piece of fooferaw have the two of you took a cotton to now?"

The girl whirled. "You mean the cotton for your shirts? The white wheat flour she saved for your biscuits while we spent the entire winter eating cheap corn tortillas?"

The jug thudded onto the table. "What's eatin' you girl, that you think you can chaw on me so right catawamptiously? It ain't fittin!" He surged from the chair, his hand raised. "I'm thinkin' you need a remembrance of who's head o' this household!"

Her lower lip curled. "That's right. Beat me. Just give me an excuse to leave. That's everything I could wish for."

He dropped his hand. "And why would you leave, girl?" He peered at her. "You find a young man to spark you while I was gone?"

She lifted her chin. "I don't need a man."

He threw back his head. "Hah! And what else you gonna go and do?" Then his face changed. "You ain't gone and done something you'll regret, have you now?"

Her lips twitched with amusement. "You might regret it," she said. "I won't be of much use to you."

He moved toward her. "What the tarnation have you gone and done?"

"You'll know when I'm ready to tell you."

As he grabbed her arm, the door opened.

"Be careful of her, por favor!" the girl's mother said as she entered. "She has been accepted into the convent in Santa Fe, to serve as a helper! Our child is a matter of grace to us now!"

The mountain man stared at his wife, then his daughter. He turned to the table. "Women!" he muttered as he lifted his jug. [5]

---

[5] Taos was famous during the trapper era for a distilled wheat-based alcohol called aguardiente, literally, "water of life" or, probably more accurately, Taos Lightning. It's said to have had quite a kick to it.

.

Lost and Found

The two trappers meet by chance in the Gila wilderness, Old One Eye Pete hunting beaver on his lonesome, the way he likes it, Marion Buckman on a scout to find his son Jedediah. Jed is with a large trapping group, out from Taos a good three months longer than expected. His father is sure in his bones that something is wrong and, against all advice, has taken out after them.

One Eye Pete is on his fourth straight day of spotting Apache sign when he comes across the elder Buckman. Given the circumstances, Pete feels right pleased to encounter another white man, despite his preference for trapping alone.

Buckman has been out six weeks. He's hunting blind at this point and is about ready to give up. Pete convinces him that there's always a chance they'll run across evidence of Jedediah's bunch up one stream or another. They might as well collect some furry bank notes while they're looking, and before the Apaches get wind of them and they're forced back to the settlements for good and all. So he and Buckman locate a likely creek in the bottom of a small canyon and follow it, watching for beaver sign.

The west end of the third pond looks promising. Pete leans his rifle and gear against a downed cottonwood and wades into the water to make the first set. He's just shoved the trap stake into place when Buckman lets out a grunt, as if someone has slugged him in the gut. Pete jerks around, his hand to the pistol at his waist, but Buckman is unhurt and staring wide-eyed at the barren ridge north of the creek.

"Apache?" Pete asks.

Buckman shakes his head, his eyes still fixed on the ridge. He takes off his hat and runs his fingers through his graying hair as he stares upward. Then he blinks and looks at Pete. "I thought—" He shakes his head again, his eyes puzzled. "I thought I saw Jed."

Pete turns and squints at the ridge with his good eye. There does appear to be something moving up there, just below the canyon's rim. Somebody hunched over and doing his best to stay below the ridgeline and unseen.

Pete moves cautiously out of the water and reaches for his rifle. "Let's just wait and see," he says.

Buckman refocuses on the ridge. "There's three of 'em. I can tell that much. And they look to be white men. See the rifles?"

Old Pete studies the side of the slope. Sunlight glints from a gun barrel. "I see one of 'em," he says.

"Injun's 'll dull down the barrel," Buckman says authoritatively. "White men like to keep 'em shiny-like. My Jed's real partic'lar 'bout that."

Pete nods and doesn't say what he's thinking—that any man fool enough to polish his rifle barrel deserves the shooting he's likely to get. Instead, he watches the men above work their way around and between the boulders scattered across the slope. As they get closer, he sees that they're dressed like white men, in woolen trousers and low moccasins, rather than Apache breech clouts and tall leg-protecting footwear.

Beside him, Marion Buckman makes a sucking sound between his teeth. "It is him!" he hisses. Then he plunges along the bank to where the stream narrows just below the beaver dam.

"You sure about that?" One Eye Pete asks. But he follows anyway. There's no sense in letting the man walk alone into a trap. After all, Buckman's concern for his son is something to admire, even if it does lead them both into danger.

Pete pauses at the base of the beaver dam and squints again at the men on the slope. The middle one raises his head and registers the trappers below. He lifts an arm and waves it wildly until the man in front of him turns and makes a warning gesture. Then the three of them go back to working their way down through the rocks.

Definitely white men. Old Pete shrugs. Unless they have Indians tracking them, he and Buckman are safe enough. And if Apaches are indeed following them, they're all in for it, anyways. He follows Buckman across the creek.

The other man is already angling through the brush toward the bottom of the ridge, on a line that will intersect the path of the descending men. Suddenly, he disappears behind a boulder twice the height of a man. Old Pete hears a voice shout "Pa!" and then silence.

When Pete rounds the big rock a few minutes later, he finds Buckman holding a younger man by the shoulders while two other men look on, their faces streaked with dirt and lank with exhaustion.

Marion Buckman turns, his face wet with tears. "My son," he says. "My Jedediah. I found him."[6]

---

[6] The Gila wilderness lies in what is today southwest New Mexico and southeast Arizona. A mountainous region with abundant wildlife, it was the home of various Apache bands, who didn't tend to appreciate the trappers' invasion of their territory in the 1820s. Old Pete had reason to be concerned about meeting them.

SMITH

They headed out of the Sangre de Cristos in mid-May, sleeting snow at their backs. They walked, all of them except the boy, and led the mules, packsaddles heavy with beaver plew. They were eight in all, counting the boy. They'd found him beside the smoking remains of a mountain cabin, the only survivor of an Indian raid. How he'd kept his scalp was a mystery to the trappers, but they shrugged at each other and agreed when Dutch George proposed that the kid come along as cook and general camp follower.

The men consisted of three Americans, two Mexicans, a half-Ute guide, and an uncommunicative grizzled-haired black man who, when they'd run across him on the Rio Colorado, had asked if they minded if he threw in with them.

The trappers had looked at each other. In fur country, a man's skin color wasn't much of an issue, and he looked honest enough, but he wasn't forthcoming about where he'd been or where he was headed, either. They'd all shrugged and he'd fallen in behind, but there was a certain amount of unease and the orphan boy was more skittish than usual, shoulders jerking at the croak of every raven overhead.

On the stranger's third night, Dutch George crouched on the opposite side of the fire and studied him for a long stretch before asking abruptly, "Ain't a runaway, are ya?"

The man was sitting on a large flat piece of sandstone, warming his hands. He looked across the flames at the German and shook his head with a small smile.

"Talkative, ain't ya?"

The man chuckled and nodded slightly.

"You been trappin' long?" Little Bill asked as he settled beside Dutch George. He was the tallest and broadest among them, though so young he didn't yet have his full beard.

The black man shrugged and stared quietly into the flames. The orphan boy came alongside him and held out a tin plate of dutch oven cornbread and stewed jerky, his twitching shoulders sloshing the food dangerously.

"Thankee," the man said, taking it. He looked at the plate thoughtfully, then began eating.

"Ya don't chow like ya been starved," George observed.

"It's good," the stranger said.

At the edge of the firelight, Webster had been trying to mend a trap. "Shit!" he said. "The dad blasted thing's completely haywire. What'd that beaver do to this thing, anyhow?"

Archuleta took the trap from Webster's hands and turned it over. "That beaver, he tried to eat him," he said. "He chew the trap jaw instead of his own leg."

"He done more to it than that," Webster said. "He twisted it a good quarter turn. I ain't never seen anything like it. And damn it to hell, that's the second one that's been shot all to pieces this trip. These contraptions'll cost me twelve dollars in Taos!"

The black man put his plate on the ground and stretched his hand toward the Mexican. Archuleta gave him the mangled trap. The stranger leaned into the firelight and examined the metal contraption carefully, then pulled a sturdy ten-inch knife from the scabbard at his waist. He used the blunt side of the blade to wedge one end of the jaw out of its stabilizing base, then began maneuvering it away from the encircling springs at either end, working the damaged bar free of the trap.

"Careful there," Dutch George said, but the black man only grunted and continued to manipulate the metal pieces.

They all watched silently as he slipped the twisted two-legged curved jaw out of the trap, then nodded to the boy. "Add some o' that fatty pine to the fire, son."

When the flames flared hot in response to the pine pitch, the stranger pulled a wad of rags from his possibles bag, wrapped it around one end of the curved metal bar, and held the skewed portion over the hottest part of the fire. For a long while, nothing happened, then the metal began to darken, redden, and finally glow white as the boy added more wood to the flames.

When the bar was hot enough, the man edged off the piece of sandstone he'd been sitting on and gingerly placed the glowing metal on it. He crouched, picked up a nearby fist-size black rock, and began tapping it against the jaw, carefully working the metal straight. "Got water?" he asked over his shoulder. The boy brought a full bucket and the man plunged the hot metal in, leaning back to avoid the hissing steam.

When the trap jaw had turned dark again, the stranger took it from the pail, returned it to the sandstone, and bent for his plate. Little Bill edged toward the rock.

"Not cool yet," the black man warned.

Hands behind his back, Bill leaned to examine the repair. "Wagh!" he said. "That should do the trick." He straightened and looked at the stranger. "Maybe you can look at the other one after you've chowed." He grinned. "Guess we can just call ya Smith."

A shadow of a smile crossed the black man's face and he nodded in agreement. From the edge of the firelight, the Indian-raid orphan boy studied him silently, shoulders still for the first time.[7]

---

[7] References to black or 'mulatto' mountain men are scattered throughout the accounts of the Americans in the Rocky Mountains. Perhaps the most famous of these men was James Beckworth, who became, like so many of the mountain men, famous both for his exploits and his capacity to stretch those experiences into memorable stories.

CULTURE CLASH

Ewing Young and his trappers were well into the Gila wilderness and moving steadily through its rocks and pines the afternoon the string of four men and three mules came into view. The strangers were working their way up a dry arroyo that intersected with Young's path.

Young held up a hand and his men all stopped in their tracks and watched the other group scramble toward them, though Enoch Jones huffed impatiently at the delay.

"Chalifoux!" Young said when the newcomers got within speaking distance. "I thought you were trapping south with James Baird."

"Baird, he is dead," the tallest of the two long-haired Frenchmen said. "La maladie, it got him."

"I'm sorry to hear that."

"We came on anyway," Chalifoux said. He gestured behind him. "Me and my brother and Grijalva and him."

The men behind Chalifoux nodded at Young politely. The youngest, the one with the dark skin and tightly-curled black hair, seemed to tense as Young's gaze landed on him, but Young only nodded absently and turned back to Chalifoux. "We've got thirty in our troop," he said. "I figure that's about all the Gila can handle at any one time. You headin' that way?"

"It is as God wills," Chalifoux said. "Perhaps to the north, toward the salt bluffs of the Navajo." He scratched his bandanna-covered forehead and nodded toward the third man in his small train. "Grijalva here, he shot a buck." He jerked his head toward the pack animal being led by the dark-skinned young man. "A good size one. You want we share the meat tonight?"

"Sure, why not?" Ewing Young grinned and jerked his head toward the end of his own train. "Fall in behind and we'll help you to cut that deer down to a more packable size."

The Frenchman's party stood and waited as Young's men filed past. The trappers eyed the dead buck with interest. A good meal of venison would make for a pleasant evening.

But it wasn't quite as pleasant as it could have been. The visitors produced whisky to accompany the meal and Enoch Jones took more than his share. Jones was apt to be more surly than usual when he drank and the presence of the young black man seemed to aggravate him.

He was leaning sullenly against a large rock that jutted from the ground a few yards beyond the fire, nursing yet another drink, when the younger man approached, a small book in his hand. The stranger crouched down beside the stones that circled the fire, opened the book, and angled its pages so the light would fall on them.

Jones scowled and leaned forward. "What're ya doin' there?" he demanded. He set his tin cup on top of the big rock, stepped forward, and nudged at the black man with his foot. "Hey! I asked a question! What're ya doin'?"

The man looked up. "I'm reading," he said. He turned the book so Jones could see the spine. "It's a play by Mr. William Shakespeare called Othello."

Jones scowled at him. "What's yer name, anyway?"

"I'm called Blackstone." The man considered Jones for a long moment, then asked. "And what is your name?"

Jones stalked away into the night. Blackstone's eyes followed him thoughtfully, then returned to his book.

But Jones was back a few minutes later, followed by Chalifoux. Jones jabbed a thumb toward Blackstone. "You see what he's doin'?" he demanded.

Chalifoux grunted. "It appears to me that he is reading." He turned away, but Jones blocked his path.

"That's illegal!" Jones said. "You can't let him do that!"

"He is a free man, Mr. Jones," Chalifoux said. "He can do as he likes."

Jones' face turned red. "He's a nigger! He ain't allowed t' read!"

Chalifoux raised an eyebrow. "This is a new law? One I know nothing of?" He turned to Blackstone. "What is this law?"

The younger man looked up, moved a small ribbon to mark his place, and closed the book. "I believe there is a law in South Carolina which makes it illegal for slaves to learn to read or write." He shifted the book into his left hand, hefting it as if its very bulk was pleasant to him. "However, as you say, I'm a free man. So the law wouldn't apply to me even if we were still in the United States."

"Which it is certain we are not," Chalifoux said. He bent, picked up a stray pine cone, and tossed it into the fire.

Blackstone glanced at Jones, then away. "And there's certainly no such law here," he said.

"Damn uppity nigger!" Jones said. He surged past Chalifoux, leaned down, and grabbed Blackstone's arm. "You talkin' back t' me?"

Blackstone rose in one easy motion, elbowing Jones aside. "I was speaking to Mr. Chalifoux," he said evenly.

Jones reached for the Shakespeare, but Blackstone lifted it out of his reach. Then Jones' foot struck sideways, into Blackstone's shin, and the younger man stumbled and lost his grip on the book, which landed, page edges down, on the stones beside the fire.

"You bastard!" Blackstone turned and shoved Jones with both hands. Jones sprawled backward, away from the fire and onto the ground beside the big rock.

Blackstone swung back to the fire and the Shakespeare, but Chalifoux had already leaned down and lifted it away from the licking flames.

As the Frenchman handed the book to Blackstone, Jones heaved himself from the ground. He was halfway to the fire again, his fists doubled and ready for battle, when Ewing Young stepped from the darkness.

"What's goin' on?" Young asked.

Jones stopped short. "Nigger bastard sucker-punched me!" he growled. He glared at Blackstone. "You ain't seen the last o' me." Then he turned and stalked into the night.

"Is he always so pleasant, that one?" Chalifoux asked Young.

Young spread his hands, palms up. "There's one in every bunch."

Chalifoux shrugged expressively, then tilted his head back to study the trees and the stars overhead. "We will move north in the morning," he said. "My party and me. To the salt bluffs, I think. They tell me they are a sight worth the seeing."[8]

---

[8] This story is a revised extract from the novel *Not Just Any Man*. One of the resources for that book is James Ohio Pattie's account of his mid 1820s adventures in the Gila wilderness, including a description of a trip 100 miles north of the Santa Rita Copper mines, in what is now southwest New Mexico, to investigate a quarter-mile long salt-imbedded bluff. Although there is little historical evidence, beyond Pattie's account, that this salt outcropping actually existed, it's the kind of thing the mountain men seem to have had a penchant for looking for. After all, salt was a commodity that could be traded along with one's furs. Mountain life wasn't all about trapping.

Naming Rights

"How old is Old Pete, anyhow?" Suzanna asks as she perches herself on a large granite rock and looks down at the valley with its long grass and meandering streams. She glances at Gerald. "He doesn't look much older than you."

Gerald chuckles. "He's been Old Pete as long as I've known him. They say Old Bill Williams started calling him that in '26 when they were trapping with St. Vrain and his bunch north of the Gila. Pete was kind of harassing Bill, wanting to know just how old he was. Finally, Old Bill got aggravated and started calling Pete 'Old Pete.'"

He grins, plucks a piece of grass, and looks it over carefully. "And that's what he's been ever since. This was a year or so before he lost his eye, or it would've probably been 'Old One Eye Pete' even then." Gerald puts the grass stem in his mouth, bites down appreciatively, and chuckles again as he gazes at the green landscape below.

"Those mountain men are quite something," Suzanna says.

"That they are," Gerald answers. "That they are."[9]

---

[9] While Suzanna, Gerald, and Old Pete are fictional characters, the trapping trip that Gerald describes actually occurred. In 1826, New Mexico's Mexican Governor Antonio Narbona signed a passport allowing Old Bill Williams, Ceran St. Vrain, and 35 other men to go to Sonora "for private trade." Instead, they trapped, focusing on the Gila River in the part of Mexican Sonora that's now Arizona in what was

---

then Apache country. During this expedition, Bill Williams, while working alone one day, was captured by Apaches, stripped naked, and turned loose in the desert. Somehow, he managed to make it 160 miles to Zuni territory and safety.

THAT'LL TEACH 'EM

Gregorio, as the youngest of the trapping expedition's camp keepers, was responsible for preparing the morning tortillas. He placed a small barrel of flour on the ground, scooped what he needed into a large wooden bowl, cut in the proper amount of fat, and mixed in water from his canteen. The mixing was more a matter of feel than attention and he glanced lazily across the campsite as he worked.

Then his head jerked. "Apache!" he exclaimed.

The trappers all turned at once. A loose line of stocky long-haired warriors stood among the rocks and pines at the far side of the clearing. The man in the center sported a large palmetto hat and a bright red long sleeved shirt. He was clearly the Chief. Three men were positioned on his left, two on his right. Another stood slightly back, an arrow fletched in his lightly-held bow.

There was a long silence. Then Ewing Young, as the trappers' leader, made a welcoming motion.

The man in the hat moved forward. He paused by the fire and looked slowly around the clearing, as if calculating the value of every item in sight, including the rifle in Thomas Smith's hands. Smith scowled and the chief permitted himself a small smile.

Then his gaze fell on Gregorio. He pointed at the barrel of flour. "Meal!" he commanded.

Ewing Young frowned, then nodded reluctantly. The Chief stepped to one side, lifted a wool blanket from a nearby rock, and flicked it open, an edge in each hand.

"That's mine!" Enoch Jones protested.

Smith jerked his head at him. "I'll give you mine," he said. Then he stepped backward into the trees and began circling toward Gregorio and the flour.

The Chief positioned himself in front of the barrel and let Jones' blanket sag slightly between his hands to form a crude container. Ewing Young waved Gregorio aside, leaned over the barrel, and began scooping out double handfuls of flour. As he dropped them into the blanket, a dusty haze rose into the morning air.

The Apache turned his head and gave his men a satisfied smile. He didn't see Thomas Smith step from the evergreens behind Gregorio, his rifle cocked and ready.

Young poured yet another double handful of flour into the blanket and held up his white-dusted palms to show that he was finished.

The Apache growled something unintelligible in response.

Young scowled and raised two fingers. "Two more," he said.

The Chief nodded and lifted the blanket slightly, ready for more.

As Young reached into the barrel again, Thomas Smith stepped past Gregorio, shoved the rifle's muzzle up under the blanket, and pulled the trigger. The bullet exploded through the cloth and blood-spattered flour splashed across the Chief's torso.

As the Apache crumpled to the ground, his men dashed into the clearing. Gunfire erupted. Arrows flew. A trapper dropped, then an Apache, then another.

Ewing Young, his upper body coated in white flour, shook his deafened head. Then an arrow flashed through the air and bit into the ground at his feet. He lunged for his rifle and aimed into the trees. But the Indians were already gone, vanished into the rocks and the pines.

Their Chief lay where he'd fallen, his red sleeves dusted with white, his chest an incongruous paste of flour and blood.

Thomas Smith stood over him. "That'll teach 'em!" he chortled. He grinned at Enoch Jones, who was crouched beside a dead Apache, the man's beaded knife sheath in his hands. "That's worth a hole in a blanket, ain't it?"

Jones grinned back at him, his eyes glittering. "Three dead, four t' go!" he agreed. "They can't be far yet."

"Three dead's enough," Ewing Young said grimly as he beat flour from his clothes. "That was a stupid stunt, Smith. You think we've seen the last of them? If that band doesn't come after us by nightfall, it'll only be because they haven't decided yet who their new leader is." His eyes glared from his white spattered head. "Next time you decide to shoot an Indian, don't do it in my face, or I may just mistake you for one."[10]

---

[10] This story is a revised extract from the novel *Not Just Any Man* and is based on an 1826 incident along the upper Gila River in what is now Arizona.

A New Life

She wasn't sure what she had been expecting, but it wasn't this. Her heart sank as she looked down at the low mud-colored town. The clouds hung low and threatening.

"Mama?"

She turned, gathering her long calico skirts in one hand and reaching for him with the other.

"Is that it?"

She nodded. They stood together, looking down. The sky grumbled again and she closed her eyes. How was she going to do this, just her and this fragile boy?

"Look!"

She opened her eyes and followed his pointing arm. The clouds had parted above the little town and a broad beam of light now danced on the houses, turning their walls golden.

She squeezed his hand and they smiled at each other. "Yes, this is it," she said. "Our new life."

~ ~ ~ ~

"I seen him! I seen him!" The boy stopped, breathless, just inside the kitchen door.

"You mean you saw him." His mother shook her head at him as she lifted the lid from the Dutch oven in the fireplace to check the biscuits. She smiled. "Who did you see?"

"Kit Carson! He was on the other side of the street, going into Padre Martinez' casa."

She nodded. "I heard this morning that he was back. What is he like?"

His shoulders sagged. "He didn't look anything like the pictures in the book Grandpa gave me when we left Kansas City."

"That was just a story," she pointed out. She turned to stir the great pot of venison stew.

"I know," he said. "But he wasn't what I expected at all. He's just a man."

~ ~ ~ ~

"I would be proud to make you my wife, Señora." Don Manuel's face was tense and pleading at the same time.

"Oh, señor," she said. "But I am a gringa. I don't know your ways. And I have a child."

"He will be to me as my child." He took her hand. "I would do my best to make you both very happy. My ranch is a beautiful place."

And that was the problem. His ranch was two days away by horseback. Her son was settled here and doing well in his studies with the Judge. What kind of future would he have if she uprooted him again?

"I'm sorry," she said.

"It is because I am Spanish."

"No! It is because of my son. I promised his dying father that he would be educated. And I cannot leave him here alone." Tears blurred her eyes as she looked up at him.[11]

---

[11] Christopher "Kit" Carson arrived in Mexican Taos in late 1826 and would go on to become known in the United States as Captain John C. Fremont's guide to California in 1844. This fame led to pulp fiction that featured Carson as a larger than life hero, a role he was uncomfortable with. The Padre Martinez mentioned here is the influential Padre Antonio José Martinez, pastor of the Taos parish from 1826 to 1857.

OLD ONE EYE PETE AND THE HALF-GROWN PUP

It's a gangly mutt, large for an Indian dog, with dirt-matted curly black hair. Old One Eye Pete looks at it in disgust as it half-crouches at his feet. It's been following him and the mule for the past two hours, ever since they left the Ute Indian encampment down canyon.

"Damned if the thing ain't smilin'," Pete mutters. He pokes the dog's side with his foot. "You a doe or a buck?" The animal rolls over obligingly, paws in the air. Buck.

Old Pete toes it again. "Well, I expect you won't last long. You'll be running off to the first camp with a bitch in heat." He turns and twitches the mule's lead rope. "Giddup."

They trail the Cimarron River up canyon through the afternoon and settle into camp under an overhanging sandstone boulder as the light begins to fade. It's still early. The sunlight goes sooner as the canyon walls narrow. But Old Pete's in no particular hurry and the pup's acting a mite tired.

"Gonna have to keep up," Pete tells it as he cuts pieces of venison off the haunch he traded from the Utes. The dog slinks toward the fire and Pete tosses it a scrap. "Too small for my roaster anyway," he mutters as he skewers a larger chunk onto a sharpened willow stick and holds it out over the flames.

~ ~ ~ ~

"Where'd that damn pup get to now?" Old Pete mutters as he and the mule reach the rocky outcropping that overlooks the valley. He can see through the ponderosa into a good stretch of grassland below, but there's no evidence of the curly-haired black Indian dog. Pete shakes his head in disgust, jams his rabbit fur hat farther down on his head, and snaps the mule's lead rope impatiently.

At least the mule doesn't need voice direction. Which is more than can be said for the dog, but Pete refuses to call the damn thing, no matter how aggravated he might feel.

Jicarilla Apaches are likely roaming the valley for elk, and Pete's taking no chance of being found before he wants to be. The dog can go to hell, for all he cares. He grunts irritably as he works his way down the hillside. Idiot pup.

He pauses at the tree line, getting his bearings, the air crisp on his face. A light snow powders the ground. A herd of perhaps thirty elk is bunched on the hillside to his left. He squints his good eye. They seem a mite restless.

Then he sees the wolves, eight or nine of them waiting downwind while two big ones trot the herd's perimeter, checking for weakness.

At his feet to his right, a low whine emanates from the prickly ground-hugging branches of a juniper bush. As Pete turns his head, the black pup eases from the grasping needles. The dog slinks to Pete's feet and crouches beside him, tail between its legs. Then it looks anxiously toward the wolves and whines again.

"Not as dumb as I took you fer," Old Pete says, adjusting his hat.

~ ~ ~ ~

There's a reason it's called Apache Canyon and Old Pete proceeds cautiously, aware that there's been a recent outbreak of hostilities between the Jicarillas and the locals. Somebody got twitchy-brained and shot off their gun without thinking twice and now the whole Sangre de Cristo range is on edge. And it doesn't matter at all that he had no part in the original quarrel.

However, Pete hasn't seen a soul in three days, and he's beginning to think he's going to get to Taos in one piece after all, if the damn half-grown dog tagging him will quit wandering off, then coming back, widening the scent trail with his idiot nosing around.

Pete scowls as the puppy reappears, this time from a thicket of scrub oak, dead leaves rattling on the ground. As the dog gets closer, it goes into a half crouch. It's holding something in its mouth and its curly black tail droops anxiously.

"What've you got there?" Pete asks. He squats and holds out his hand, and the dog releases the item into his palm. "Shit!" Pete says, dropping it.

Then he leans closer and sniffs. It really is shit. Human, too. Fresh enough to still stink. He rises, studying the slopes on either side, turning to examine the Pass behind him. So much for being alone.

"Thankee, pup," he mutters. "I think."

Well Cultivated

From the garden on the slope in front of the house, Suzanna had an unimpeded view of the Moreno Valley for a good two miles in each direction, so when she looked up from hoeing the potato patch and glanced south, she immediately spotted the man and horse cresting the rise on the road from Mora and Taos.

He was on foot, leading a horse, and carrying a gun. Suzanna frowned. Why wasn't the gun in a saddle scabbard? Was he expecting trouble? Hunting? Or hunting trouble, rather than waiting for it? She thumped the flat of the hoe against a clump of dirt, considering. Her husband Gerald and his father had headed to Taos the day before and there was only herself, the children, and Ramón, the cook/handyman, on the place. Eight-year-old Andrew was at the bottom of the potato patch, dreamily raking together the weeds she'd hoed up. "Where's Alma?" Suzanna called to him.

The child hesitated. "I think she went fishing."

Suzanna shook her head. Alma was always looking for fish. Suzanna wished Gerald Sr. had never rigged that girl a fishing pole. She shaded her eyes, looking south again. The man was dropping off the ridge and it was difficult to make him out against the browning hillside, but she could see that he was still walking. And still carrying the rifle.

She turned toward the cabin. Ramón was in the doorway. He looked at her with a slight frown. "I do not know him," he said. "Or the horse he is leading."

There were few people or horses in nuevomexico that Ramón Chavez didn't know, even from a distance, and fewer the man was not related to in some way. His roots were both Spanish and Pueblan, well cultivated and deep. He frowned again, gazing at the walker and his horse. "I think he is not coming here," he said. "I think he travels north."

Suzanna studied Ramón, wondering how he knew these things. But she'd never known him to be wrong and she turned back to her work. "I do wish Alma would stay closer to home," she muttered as she whacked the corner of the hoe sharply downward on a particularly stubborn section of invading grass.

Ramón turned to Andrew. "And where is your sister?" he asked.

Andrew gestured southward. "She said she saw trout in Six Mile Creek yesterday."

~ ~ ~ ~

Alma had been resting face down in the browning grass beneath one of the golden narrow leaf cottonwoods that clustered beside the creek. When she lifted her drowsy head, she saw the man and roan stallion on the rise south of the creek, and was glad she'd resisted her mother's enthusiasm for the red dress that morning. Alma didn't like to wear bright colors. They spooked the fish and wild turkey. She studied the man coming down the hill. He didn't look dangerous. But it was odd that he was leading the horse and carrying his rifle. Was he hunting something Alma couldn't see?

She turned her head slowly, studying the autumn landscape. The only animals evident were three black-spotted cows, straying once again from the cabin pasture. Alma grimaced, knowing she and Andrew would be sent to fetch them when Ramón realized they were gone.

If she stayed still and didn't look directly at the man with the gun, there was little danger he'd see her, she told herself. She'd learned about not looking too long at someone whose attention you wanted to avoid. Her grandfather had taught her that. He was smart, her grandfather. Suddenly, the roan stumbled, and she realized why the man was afoot. The stallion was lame.

Alma frowned. The man seemed to be heading straight north, studiously avoiding even a glance toward the cabin perched on the hillside at the head of Cimarron canyon. You'd think he'd want some assistance with the roan—help with replacing a shoe or just a place to rest up while his mount healed.

They were almost abreast of her now, crossing the stream where it curved across the dirt track and darkened the soil and rocks. She could see now that he was an americano like her mother's father, the travel dust making his face seem harsh and old but emphasizing the sky blue of his eyes. Without quite knowing why, the girl flattened further into the grass.

Then man and horse moved off the road toward the creek and Alma's hiding place. She flicked her eyes away, then back, trying to look without staring. The man released the roan's reins and, right hand still clutching his rifle, crouched beside the creek and fumbled at the canteen that hung from a rawhide thong at his belt. Finally, he got it open and into the running water.

The stallion took the opportunity to drink also, keeping his left foreleg carefully positioned so as not to put any pressure on it. Reddish black stuff oozed just above the inside of its knee. Alma frowned. Had it been cut or was that a scrape from a stray bullet?

But then the man straightened and in one fluid motion released the canteen and aimed his rifle squarely at Alma's cottonwood. "You come on outta there real easy now," he said, voice raspy from lack of use. "An' keep your hands away from your sides while you're at it."

Alma's mouth twitched in disgust. She'd been so intrigued by the horse's wound that she'd forgotten to break her gaze. She raised herself slowly and moved her hands, palms forward, away from her skirts. "I don't have a weapon, mister," she said. She nodded at the grass beside her. "Except for my fishing pole."

The man jerked his head northward. "You connected with that cabin?"

"Yes, sir."

He stared at her for a long moment, then lowered the rifle. "You're mighty young to be wanderin'."

Alma lifted her ten-year-old chin and didn't answer. It was none of his business how old she was.

"Who's at your place?"

"Ramón Chavez," she said. "He used to be a mountain man. And he's just as good a shot now as he was then."

The man's eyes narrowed. "Ain't no mexicano mountain men."

She shrugged. "That's what most americanos think."

He squinted as if trying to understand the disdain for American sensibilities in a girl who spoke such clear English, then turned and spat. He glanced in the direction of the cabin, then narrowed his blue eyes at her again. "No one else there?"

"My pa and my grandpa'll be back before sundown," she said, suddenly cautious.

"This Ramón know how to doctor horses?"

"Ramón knows just about everything."

He made a sound as if he wanted to chuckle but had forgotten how. "Well, show me the way then," he said.

She glanced at the cottonwood. "I need to get my fishing pole." She gestured toward the stream. "And my fish."

Alma was rather proud of the five ten-inch trout she'd caught that morning, but the man made no comment when she returned from the stream. He simply gestured with the rifle barrel for her to walk in front of him.

She did so, but moved casually to one side, giving herself a chance to flatten into the grass and rocks if he pointed the gun more aggressively. She bit her lip, wondering what her mother would say when she arrived home like this.

But then a shape appeared around a small hill just east of the road, and Ramón was coming toward them, shotgun casually tilted over his shoulder, a dog at his heels as if he were out hunting quail. Alma's chest loosened.

"Buenos días," Ramón said to the man with the roan stallion. He nodded at Alma. "Those are good fish," he said. "Go now. Your mother waits."

The traveler's eyes squinted as if in objection, but the old man's shotgun moved slightly from his shoulder, as if he tested its heft. "You have need of assistance?" Ramón asked the stranger as Alma moved past him. "It appears your horse has experienced an injury."

~ ~ ~ ~

Her mother was tight-lipped when Alma reached home. "Five trout!" Alma said brightly, as she stood at the edge of the potato patch. "Ten inches!"

Suzanna whacked at another weed with the blade of her hoe. "Go inside," she said. She moved away to deal with another clump of pigweed.

Andrew had stopped his work and was watching. Alma looked at him beseechingly, but he shrugged and shook his head. Their mother was in no mood to be sweet-talked. Better to lay low for a while.

Alma left the cleaned fish in a bucket of water in the lean-to kitchen and climbed into the loft. When she came back down in the red dress, her mother was standing at the kitchen table, drying her hands. "If you think wearing that dress is going to placate me, you are very much mistaken, young lady."

"I was only fishing."

"At Six Mile Creek, which is entirely too far out of sight or earshot. And with nothing but a fishing pole for protection." Suzanna tossed the towel onto the table. Her hands went to her hips. "How many times must I remind you that you are not a boy?"

The sound of men's voices came suddenly from the yard. Alma darted gratefully into the central part of the cabin and opened the door as the men stepped onto the porch.

"Wait!" her mother said sharply, but Ramón was already ushering the traveler into the house.

"I was mistaken," he told Suzanna apologetically. "This is Arthur Chesterfield, the primo of my nephew's daughter's husband."

Suzanna's lips twitched. The man really *was* related to everyone in nuevomexico. But that still didn't completely ease her anxiety. She glanced at the rifle in the stranger's right hand.

Chesterfield's gaze followed hers, then he turned to the door and leaned the gun carefully against the wall. "I was keepin' it outa the scabbard to try and relieve the pressure on Stanley's leg," he said, his voice still gravelly.

Suzanna raised an eyebrow. "Stanley?"

"The roan," the man replied, and Alma stifled a giggle. Stanley the Stallion. The americano had a sense of humor.

"You'll want to clean up," Suzanna said briskly. She looked toward the half-open front door and raised her voice. "Andrew, please draw more water." She turned to Ramón. "Alma left the trout in the kitchen."

A smile flashed across the old man's face and he nodded. "The cows have gone loose again," he told her.

Suzanna turned to Alma. "After Andrew has drawn the water, you and he will retrieve those cows," she said severely. "Do *not* go after them by yourself, young lady. You've done quite enough wandering for one day."

Beaver Tale

The yearling beaver is hungry, but when he tries to filch a piece of tender green shoot from his infant siblings, his mother hisses sharply. He moves toward the lodge's diving hole, but his father blocks the way and chitters at him. The yearling slinks to one side of the den and begins grooming his fur with his right hind foot. The divided nail on his second toe makes for a kind of comb that simplifies this process considerably.

There are three new kits this spring, which keep his parents busy. His father moves to help with the feeding and the yearling sees his chance. He slides into the diving hole and out into the pond.

The sky is bright overhead. The beaver dives, but not before the one-eyed man on the bank nudges the young girl beside him. "See, I told you that ole lodge was still occupied!" he says gleefully.

~ ~ ~ ~

"Old Pete ain't gonna trap it, is he?" Andrew whispers. The two children are crouched on the edge of the beaver pond, peering at the yearling beaver feeding on the opposite bank.

"He says he needs a new hat and beaver tail is mighty tasty," Alma answers.

"He don't need a new hat!" Andrew says loudly. There's a slapping sound on the water to their left, and the yearling turns and slides into the pond.

"I didn't even see the other one," Andrew says sorrowfully.

"Should of kept your voice down." Alma stands up.

"How can you watch them like you do and not worry about Old Pete trapping them?"

She shrugs. "Everything dies. Mama says it's all part of God's plan." She moves away, toward the rocky path that leads up the Cimarron River toward home.

"Old Pete don't need a new hat," Andrew insists as he follows.

~ ~ ~ ~

"Beaver tail is almighty tasty," Old Pete observes as he sits on the front porch whittling a stick.

Andrew scowls. "Papa says it's all fat and grease. Not good at all."

"Fat tastes plenty good when you've been eating venison and elk a long spell. Wild game's almighty lean."

"You've been eating here," Andrew insists. "We've got plenty of fat from the hogs."

Andrew's mother comes out of the house. "The kindling box is empty," she tells him.

He rises obediently and heads toward the woodpile.

"Are you still teasing him about trapping that beaver?" she asks Old Pete.

The trapper grins. "He's a right risible youngster, ain't he?"

"Who admires you, although I can't think why," she says tartly. "He's beginning to believe that men kill for the sheer pleasure of it."

Old Pete grunts and tosses his stick to the ground. "Think I'll help with that kindling," he says.

~ ~ ~ ~

"I ain't gonna place a trap for that beaver, son." Old Pete and the boy are resetting a garden fence post. Andrew holds it steady as Old Pete shovels dirt into the hole.

"Alma said you need a new hat."

Pete chuckles. "Hat's good for another season or two."

"But what then?"

"Somethin'll turn up."

"You said beaver tail was tasty."

Old Pete leans on his shovel. "Funny thing about that. Only really tasted good when there was plenty to trap and the peltries were selling high." He begins tamping down the dirt around the post with his foot. "You think this'll be strong enough to keep those elk out?"

"I hope so. Mama got pretty mad at them last spring. She was out here with the shotgun, but Papa says all she did was give them a scare. They'll be back when they're hungry enough."[12]

---

[12] A beaver litter can range from one to four kits. The mother nurses them for the first two weeks, then the parents feed them leafy twigs until the babies are two or three months old. Two year old beavers will often stay with their parents to help raise new litters, postponing their own mating and reproduction until age three. The yearling in this story isn't as helpful.

TOO EASY

From his position on the flat adobe rooftop, U.S. Brigadier General Stephen Kearny could see the entire plaza and all the people in it. And the people of Las Vegas, in the Mexican departamento de nuevomexico, now an American possession, could see him.

Kearny studied their carefully blank faces, then turned and looked at the three Mexican officials standing behind him. Their eyes were firmly fixed on the roof's dirt-packed surface.

The General faced the plaza again. He cleared his throat, raised the pages of his speech, and began to read, pausing periodically to allow the Mexican interpreter to translate. "I have come amongst you by the orders of my government," he declared. "To take possession of your country and extend over it the laws of the United States. We consider it, and have done so for some time, a part of the territory of the United States."

As he waited for the translator, Kearny examined the plaza. It wasn't much. A dusty square surrounded by low-slung mud brick buildings. The faces of the people below were the same color as the buildings. And they looked just as blank. As if their very souls were shuttered. The only sound was a light clunk, as the wind moved the hardware on the flag pole he'd had set up at one end of the plaza.

The interpreter finished and Kearny went back to his speech. "Henceforth, I absolve you from all allegiance to the Mexican government," he announced. "And from all obedience to General Armijo. He is no longer your Governor." That got their attention. Heads snapped toward him, though the faces were still carefully blank.

The General waited for some kind of sound, either of approbation or dissent, but there was only the dull clunk of metal against empty flagpole. He raised his voice. This next section was the part he'd been told was most important. "Some of your priests have told you all sorts of stories," he began.

The interpreter paused, as if not certain how to express this, but the General gave him a stern look. The man nodded anxiously and said a few words in Spanish, then Kearny plunged on.

"My government respects your religion as much as the Protestant religion, and allows each man to worship his Creator as his heart tells him is best," he said firmly. "Its laws protect the Catholic as well as the Protestant."

Below, unblinking black eyes gazed up at him. Kearny shook his head in exasperation, then went on with his speech.

As he finished saying, "I respect a good Catholic as much as a good Protestant," a troop of his soldiers marched into the far side of the square. They halted and wheeled to face him, stiff with military alertness. Their Lieutenant snapped off a salute.

Kearny permitted himself a small smile. The Lieutenant had timed his entrance well. As Kearny returned the salute, the citizens below twisted around to follow his gaze. They all watched as the Lieutenant barked a command and two men stepped out from the troop and moved to the flag pole. The rest of the soldiers turned and marched briskly out of the plaza, toward the road to Santa Fe.

"There goes my army!" Kearny said, trying to keep the triumph out of his voice. "You see but a small portion of it. There are many more behind." He leaned forward slightly. "Resistance is useless."

The faces lifted toward him again and Kearny forced himself not to lean back and away from them. The rooftop was suddenly unpleasantly warm, in spite of the breeze.

Abruptly, he turned to the Mexican officials—the town's mayor and two militia captains. It was time to administer their oaths of allegiance to the United States and get on with his mission.

The General rattled off the words, almost not caring if these dusty Mexicans understood what he said or what he was demanding of them, or if the interpreter had time to fully translate each phrase before Kearny moved on to the next one.

The journey here had been pleasant enough. The prairies were rich with grass, the mountains a sight for sore eyes after the monotonous plains. But the routine quality of the expedition was something of a disappointment, especially after news began to filter in from Zachary Taylor's campaign into Mexico from Texas. Kearny wanted that kind of glory.

He pulled his attention back to the task at hand and finished administering the oaths. Then he nodded to the two soldiers standing next to the flag pole and stood at attention as they raised the Stars and Stripes over the first New Mexico town to be so honored.

The breeze caught the flag and it flared boldly against the turquoise sky and brown buildings. Kearny's heart lifted, in spite of the resounding silence from the citizens below. He'd get this over quickly and move on to California. Perhaps that conquest would be more exciting. Or—the thought rose unbidden—perhaps the news from the Santa Fe merchants was incorrect. Perhaps the arrangements with New Mexico's Governor Armijo would fall through and the two forces would engage after all.

It wasn't that he necessarily wanted to do battle with New Mexico's militia. But this mute acceptance of the U.S. Army's presence was unnerving. It was too easy. Kearny looked again at the Las Vegas citizens and their impassive faces, then turned and moved across the flat roof toward the rickety ladder to the street and his waiting men. He forced himself not to move too quickly. After all, he didn't want to look as if he was beating a retreat. [13]

---

[13] On August 15, 1846, U.S. Brigadier General Stephen Watts Kearny stood on the flat roof of a building on the Las Vegas, New Mexico plaza and informed the people below that they were now living in the United States. There are various versions of the speech he gave that day. This story uses the one reported by Ralph Emerson Twitchell in *The Leading Facts of New Mexico History,* Vol. 2.

Governor Manuel Armijo initially deployed 3,000 militia troops to block the U.S. Army's route to Santa Fe. However, Armijo, who'd diffused a bloody revolt almost ten years earlier through diplomacy, seems to have not had the heart for battle. He ordered his militia to disband and headed to central Mexico. At the time, it was rumored that financial inducements from American merchants in Santa Fe facilitated this course of action. Others asserted that Armijo was truly a man of peace and didn't wish to see his people slaughtered.

Kearny's triumph really *was* too easy. Although there was no resistance to his troops when they entered New Mexico in the summer of 1846, revolt broke out in Taos and Mora early the following year. Kearny was in California by then, and missed that particular excitement.

THEY WERE MY FRIENDS

"I saw them kill the two young ones," her brother says. Andrew glances at Alma, then at Old Pete smoking his pipe on the other side of the fireplace. "It's been an entire year, but sometimes it feels like it just happened."

He leans from his chair to add another log to the fire. "Narciso Beaubien and Manuelito seem so young to me now. But I was only a year older." He shakes his head. "I think Manuel realized what was happening, but Chicho didn't seem to. I suppose he'd forgotten a good deal while he was at that school in Missouri. He was remembering only the good things about Taos, about nuevomexico."

"And much had changed since Narciso left for school." Alma lifts her sewing from the work basket beside her chair. "After the American troops arrived."

Andrew nods. "It did, didn't it? Everything shifted pretty quickly in the five months after General Kearny marched in."

"So you saw what happened in the Beaubien shed?" Old Pete asks.

Alma looks up, then back down at her work. She's been afraid to ask this question. As close as she and her brother are, the details of what he experienced that day in early 1847 have seemed untouchable. But she wants so badly to know. She's heard only rumors. No one will talk about it, especially with a woman. An American one, at that. The fact that she was born and raised here in New Mexico is irrelevant in the current environment. Even after a year, the tensions are still there. There's still a sense of shock at what happened that January day, the ferocity of the American response.

Andrew picks up the fire iron and maneuvers a log closer to the center of the flames. He glances at Old Pete, then away. "Chicho and Manuelito followed me into the shed. I thought we'd be safer there." He studies the flames. "I pushed them in ahead of me, then I dove behind the wagon and started piling straw over myself. I was hissing at them to hide when the door opened." He turns his head and stares at the darkening window.

There's a long silence. Alma looks at him, as manly and beautiful as ever in the firelight. The broad shoulders, the brown skin darkened and the blond hair lightened from exposure to the sun. But he's changed in the last year. Since the shed. His eyes are sadder now, his mouth guarded. Her sweet baby brother. She has a sudden urge to reach out and touch his hair, pull his forehead to her and kiss it the way she did when they were children. But that brother is gone now. There's no returning to what once was.

Then Andrew begins again, his voice flat. "I was crouched down behind the wagon, but I could see well enough through the cracks in the side boards. Manuel was moving toward me when Old Man Ysidro yanked the door open, and Manuel turned around and went back to Chicho. The old man had a stick in his hand as thick as my wrist. Javier was right behind him."

Andrew looks at Alma. "You know how tall Javier is. He was looking over Ysidro's shoulder." He pauses. "Chicho always liked Javier. They were good friends before Chicho left for school."

His voice changes. "Or so I thought. Chicho smiled the way he always did, so delighted to see a friend, and moved toward Javier with his hand out."

Andrew glances at Old Pete, then looks into the fire. "Old Man Ysidro hit him on the head with the stick. He just lifted it and swung sideways and crashed the stick into Chicho's skull. Chicho crumpled, straight down." Andrew swallows, the firelight glinting on his throat. "He didn't fall over. He just collapsed."

He turns his head and goes on talking, but more to the window than to the others. "Then they all came crowding into the shed and I couldn't see what was happening, but there was a kind of gasping sound and I could see blood spurting. I thought I was going to be sick. Everything went silent. Someone at the back growled 'Vi tres' and I was sure I was next, but then a man outside yelled, 'They got Bent!' and they all took off." Andrew blinks. "When I came out from behind the wagon, I saw they were both dead. Their throats had been slit."

There's a long pause, then Andrew turns his head and gives Alma a stricken look. "They were my friends and I didn't help them. I hid while they died."

Alma's fingertips grip the fabric in her lap as if they're afraid to let go. "You would have been killed too," she says. She swallows and looks into his eyes. "The mob was too big and too wild. You couldn't have saved either of those boys."

"I tell myself that. Every night." He raises a shoulder. "Every day. But even after all this time, it still doesn't help."

There's a long silence. Alma lifts her sewing from her lap, but the light from the window has dimmed too much and the fire has died down too far. Her eyes sting and she can't see her stitches anymore.

"Javier was my friend," her brother says. "And Chicho. Manuelito, too. Though he was more Chicho's friend than mine."

"You lost so much that day," Alma says, knowing how inadequate this is.

"We all did." A note of bitterness creeps into his voice. "Except Javier."

Old Pete removes his pipe from his mouth. "Javier too," he says.

Andrew grunts and stands up. "I'm going out to close up the barn."

Alma nods. As he leaves the cabin, she begins folding her sewing into her basket.

"That was Javier's uncle that was leadin' the mob at the shed," Old Pete says. "The one Carlos Beaubien kicked out of his store for stealin' that sugar."

She looks up in surprise. "That was five years ago."

"He always did have a good memory, that one. Especially for anything he took as an insult."

"From what I heard at the time, Charles Beaubien overreacted. Pablo Ysidro hadn't stolen a thing." Alma looks into the fire for a long moment, then sighs. "Life gets so complicated."

"It does at that," Old Pete says. He shakes his head and studies the dying fire. "It does at that."[14]

---

[14] Although the people in this story are fictional, the events that Andrew describes are not. When U.S. Brigadier General Stephen W. Kearny pushed on to California from New Mexico in late 1846, he left behind a military outpost in Santa Fe and a provisional government headed by Virginia-born Taos merchant Charles Bent. An insurrection against the new American government erupted in Taos and Mora in mid January 1847 and Bent and at least twelve others were killed. Among the dead were 14-year-old Narciso 'Chicho' Beaubien, who had just returned from school in St. Louis, and one of his friends. The accounts differ regarding the name and ethnicity of his friend.

WELL FOUNDED PESSIMISM

The dark-skinned young woman and the old Ute man sat with the quietness of old friends on the cabin porch, out of the bright mountain sun.

Stands Alone gazed at the green-black slopes lining the opposite side of the long grassy valley. "My people have no other options," he said bleakly.

Alma tucked a wayward black curl behind her right ear. "Surely there is somewhere you can go to live your lives in peace."

The old man shook his head. "Wherever we go, the whites follow and take the little we possess."

"Not all of us."

A small smile crossed his seamed face. "You, my friend, are not white. Your people have also known sorrow and theft."

The young woman raised an eyebrow, but could not contradict. There was slavery in her veins, if not her experience, though, with enough face powder, she could pass for a deeply tanned white woman. Only the pale splotches on her cheeks, where the pigmentation wasn't consistent, gave her away. Her French/Navajo/American mother had applied various potions in her attempt to even out the child's skin tone, but nothing had worked and after her mother's death, Alma had stopped trying.

"You and your people could hunt here," she said now, gesturing toward the valley. "After all, it was your land before my parents arrived."

"It was," Stands Alone agreed. "And the hunting rights are still ours. Your father and I made an agreement that allowed him his pastures. And those men who the Mexican government gave the land to also agreed, that Carlos Beaubien and his friend Don Guadalupe Miranda."

His gaze moved toward the north end of the valley, where another cabin was under construction behind a screen of tree-covered hills. "As they in turn have allowed others." The old man shook his head. "As still others will come. And they will not ask permission."

Alma nodded, silent before the Ute's well-founded pessimism. Since the American takeover in 1846, eastern settlers had moved steadily into New Mexico Territory. Eventually, they would find even this protected valley, which she now shared with only her brother, the former nuevomexicano mountain man Ramón who acted as their cook and handyman, and the occasional band of Indian hunters or herders from Taos. Judge Beaubien never came to the valley and Don Miranda had long since returned to Mexico, where he was born.

"It is not for myself that I dread this move the American government is forcing upon us," the Ute elder said. "But the land to which they send us is unfamiliar, and the young men are angry and uncontrollable. They talk of war against all who have built houses on our land. I fear even for you."

Alma frowned. "We have always lived in peace with both the Ute and the Apache," she said. "We have endeavored not to encroach on the hunting grounds or to frighten off the elk and the deer."

The old man chuckled. "I recall that your mother was not always happy about that."

Alma grinned. "She was set on growing corn up here, even if it killed her and all the beasts who wanted to eat it."

"A determined woman," Stands Alone said.

Alma nodded somberly, then turned back to the subject at hand. "If the young men come, my brother and I will treat them with respect."

"May they respond with respect," he said prayerfully.

"We will remain vigilant," she told him. "The rifles will be ready, if need be." She shook her head, dark eyes somber. "Although I pray it will not come to that."

"Your brother will protect you," the old man said, reassuring himself as much as her. "And Ramón."

But when the young men came three days later, neither Andrew nor Ramón were at hand.

Ramón had headed north after three stray cows and Andrew was in a side canyon checking his rabbit snares. So the house was quiet when Alma looked up from her book to see a Ute man with a red stripe of paint down one side of his face peering through the small window at the front of the cabin.

A spasm of fear clutched Alma's belly and her mother's exasperated voice echoed in her memory: "It's dangerous for a woman in this god forsaken valley!" Then the rich voice of her father's father reminded her: "People are like dogs. They'll sense your fear if you let yourself feel it."

Alma took a deep breath, steadying herself. Then she stood, crossed the room, lifted the always-loaded shotgun from the wall, and swung the cabin door firmly open.

Ten young braves stood in the yard, their faces striped with the Utes' signature red war paint, chests bared for battle.

"Hello," Alma said, the shotgun under her arm. "How are you all today?" The words seemed inadequate, but she thought the tone was firm enough. She knew most of them: the grandson of Stands Alone, two of the grandson's cousins, and several others whose faces she recognized. At the back of the group, toward the long low adobe-and-timber barn, was Running Wolf, who as a boy had taught Alma's brother how to set the snares he was now checking.

"We are not well," the grandson of Stands Alone said. "We are unhappy."

"I am sorry to hear that," Alma said calmly.

"You whites have come in and now we have no game," the warrior behind him said. This was a man Alma didn't know. A broad stripe of red ran down each cheek, flattening the planes of his cheekbones.

A young boy came running from the barn, eyes bright with excitement. "There are no men here," he told the broadly-painted one breathlessly. "And there are cattle!"

The man nodded, his eyes on Alma's shotgun.

One of the grandson's cousins chuckled and shifted a hatchet from his left hand to his right. "The woman has a good shape," he observed.

"We will have her and then we will burn the house and take the cattle," the broadly-striped one announced. He took a step forward and raised his voice. "Then we will feast!"

Alma's stomach tightened. She lifted the shotgun, sighting on the man's chest. "But you yourself will not have me, and you will not feast!" she said sharply. "You will be dead!"

An irritated growl swept across the yard. At the corner of her eye, Alma saw the cousin easing around the corner of the cabin, toward the lean-to kitchen's door. Had she barred it after she came in from the outhouse? Alma forced her gaze to remain on the broadly-painted man's bare chest, her shotgun barrel steady.

"I would not touch her," a disgusted voice said from the back of the crowd. Running Wolf? She didn't move her eyes. "Those spots on her face are the sign of disease. Smallpox or something worse."

The broadly-painted one peered sharply into Alma's face and she nodded. "That's right!" she said, meeting his eyes defiantly. "I will shoot you and you will die quickly." She raised her voice. "But if these others are loco enough to have me, they will suffer for a long time before they die." She chuckled grimly. "I will take all of you with me! And you will die the painful and lingering death of disease, not of battle!"

A confused murmur passed over the yard. Alma held the shotgun muzzle steady on the broadly-painted man's chest. There was a long silence, then the other cousin jerked his head toward the barn. "We will take cattle instead," he pronounced. "The cattle are not diseased."

"Two fat cows to feed us and our children." Running Wolf moved slightly forward. His eyes swept the cluster of warriors, then turned toward the barn. "We will all feast this night!"

The warriors swung to face the barn and Alma eased backward into the house. She shoved the door closed, then leaned against it, heart pounding her ribs, fingers cramped painfully on the gunstock. Then she crept to the kitchen, assured herself that the door was indeed barred, and slipped back into the front room. She sank into her mother's old rocking chair and placed the shotgun gently on the floor beside her. Only when she heard Ramón and Andrew on the porch did she lift her hands from her face, now splotchy with tears.[15]

---

[15] In 1841, the Mexican government granted Charles 'Carlos' Beaubien and Guadalupe Miranda a vast tract of land east of Taos that included all of what is today Colfax County, New Mexico. Beaubien tried to settle the land on a share system with anyone willing to farm or raise livestock there. His son-in-law Lucien B. Maxwell was the collection agent. Families such as Alma and her brother shared the land with the Ute and Jicarilla Apache bands that had been living and hunting in the Sangre de Cristo mountains and the plains to the east since prior to the arrival of the Spanish.

DECISIONS

The four young people stood inside the ranch cabin's newly whitewashed walls and looked at each other uncertainly.

"What will you do?" Andrew asked. His sister Alma frowned at him, but Kathy only shook her carefully braided blond head, white handkerchief to her blue eyes.

William went to the window. A line of Taos Pueblo riders moved steadily toward the cabin through the gap from the southern part of the valley. "Here they come," he said. He turned to his sister. "You gave your word."

Kathy nodded, then shook her head. "Not precisely," she whispered.

"I beg your pardon?"

Kathy lifted her head. "I didn't say that I would marry Peter," she said. "I didn't say those precise words. But I'm sure that's what he understood me to say."

William's jaw tightened under his reddish-blond beard. "And you didn't disabuse him of that notion, either. And agreed in some way to a date."

She turned away, to the only other woman in the room. "Oh, Alma, what am I going to do?"

The dark-haired, deeply tanned, and sturdy Alma put her arms around her pale thin blond friend. "You should follow your heart," she said, feeling the inadequacy of her words.

Kathy shook her head against Alma's shoulder. "I don't know," she sobbed. "I'm so afraid."

Andrew was at the window now. "You'll need to decide pretty quickly," he said. "They're almost here."

But by the time the Taos Pueblo party rode into the dirt and gravel yard, Kathy had disappeared out the cabin's back door. William and Andrew moved outside to provide an initial greeting and deal with the animals. Alma took a deep breath and faced the doorway, her square brown face anxious. She tucked an unruly curl behind her right ear.

Peter entered first, his dark face bright as an expectant schoolboy's. He wore a blue and white checked shirt and pants so new they still had fold creases across the thighs. He took one look at Alma's face and his expression fell. He moved to the far wall and faced it quietly, dark head bowed.

Several children followed him inside and Alma scooped up a three-year-old boy she'd never seen before. "Where'd you get those big gray eyes?" she asked him. He giggled and she held him to her chest as Peter's father, Oscar came through the doorway. He was dressed in traditional Taos garb, long hair tucked into a bun at the nape of his neck.

"Who is this little man?" she asked. "I haven't met him before."

Oscar's eyes swept around the whitewashed room and came to rest on his son, face to the wall. "He's my wife's nephew's child," he answered. "The one who married the half-French girl." He turned to the two men who had followed him in and shook his head slightly.

The men turned and headed back to the yard, shutting the door behind them. Oscar glanced at Peter, then Alma. "And where is my son's Katarina?"

Alma's eyes dropped and she set the little boy on the floor. He looked up at the two adults uncertainly, then he and the other children moved to the door.

Oscar let them out, then turned back to Alma. "Is there a problem?" His voice was mild enough, but there was an edge to it, as if he already knew the answer to his question.

"There has been a misunderstanding," Alma said.

Peter made a muffled sound and turned to face them, slim body tense. "There has been no misunderstanding." He looked at his father. "I have built us a house. Katarina may have misunderstood, but I did not."

Oscar's jaws tightened. "It is because we are Pueblan."

Alma shook her head and spread her hands, palms up. "It is simply a misunderstanding. Perhaps some confusion of languages."

"There has been no confusion," Peter said stiffly.

"Come, my son," Oscar said. "We will not waste our words on this matter."

"I am so very sorry," Alma said helplessly.

Oscar nodded slightly, acknowledging her words as he turned away. Peter, on the other hand, scowled into her face before he followed his father from the cabin and its mocking white walls.

Alma stood in the center of the room for a long time, eyes closed against the windowed sunlight, grieving for the pain in Peter's face, the controlled anger in Oscar's. Oscar had been her father's good friend. Would he ever forgive her for her part in this?

In the yard, men's voices muttered and horse hooves stirred the gravelly dirt. A child asked a plaintive question, then the group from the Pueblo was gone.

Alma slipped out the back to look for Kathy and found her hunched on a small boulder on the hillside, staring south at the receding horses, her face wet with tears. "Oh, Alma, what have I done?" she asked plaintively. "I have hurt him so much."

"It's better to hurt him now than to live a lifetime of misery together," Alma said stoutly.

Kathy shook her head. "It would not have been a complete misery."

"I told him there had been a misunderstanding."

Kathy nodded, her eyes still focused on the horses moving steadily toward the lower Moreno Valley, where they would cross Palo Flechado Pass and move west down the Rio Fernando valley, then north through the village of Don Fernando de Taos to the multi-storied five-hundred-year-old pueblo. "Misunderstanding is certainly the appropriate word," she said ruefully.

Alma looked away, studying the creek bed below and the cattle in the rich grass beside it. It was fine ranch land, this upper section of the Moreno Valley. Richer in some ways than the land she and her brother ranched in the lower part of the valley. The Taos Valley was well enough. It certainly had beautiful pasture land. But it was dryer there, and hotter in summer. It wasn't the Moreno, with its green, high-mountain beauty, narrow meandering streams, and cool summer breezes. If she were Kathy, it would be hard indeed to leave such a place.

But then Kathy took a deep, ragged breath. "I have misunderstood my own heart," she said. "And angered and insulted Peter's family. Oscar is a proud man and his wife is even prouder. She dislikes me because I am not Pueblan. Now she will have even more reason to object to me." She turned to her friend, tears welling again. "Oh, Alma, what have I done? They will never forgive me for this!"

~ ~ ~ ~

Three weeks later Kathy paid an unexpected visit to the lower valley. Alma was in the bare yard of the cabin she shared with her brother on the hillside overlooking the head of the Cimarron Canyon, but for once she was paying no attention to the scenic valley below. Instead, she was carefully following the directions of the old curandera Guadalupita Otero, learning to make soap from yucca roots.

As they did every summer, the Taos folk healer and her son's family had camped at the eastern end of Six Mile Creek, southwest of Alma and Andrew's cabin, to graze their sheep and goats and enjoy the cool mountain air. The day before, Alma had happened upon Guadalupita on a nearby hillside, struggling to carry a large basket of yucca roots.

As they carried the basket between them down the slope, the old woman had explained that she would make soap from the roots and Alma had asked to be taught the process. Now they were carefully chopping the peeled and slippery chunks and mixing them into a pot of water simmering over a fire in the yard.

When Kathy arrived, they took a break inside, out of the sun, and Alma used a bit of precious sugar to sweeten the wild mint tea she'd brewed that morning. "I haven't had time to chill it in the stream," she apologized.

"It is better for you warm," Guadalupita said.

Kathy nodded absently. She sipped her tea and looked at the floor.

"How is everything up at the ranch?" Alma asked. She looked more closely at her friend and the pensive tilt of her blond head. "Are you well?"

Kathy looked up and glanced from Alma to the old lady, then to Alma again.

"Claramente, this is a private matter, " Guadalupita said. She set down her cup and pushed herself to her feet. "We can finish the soap another day." She turned to Alma. "Finish adding the amole to the water and then…"

"Please stay, señora," Kathy said. She leaned forward and looked into the old woman's face. "I may need your assistance. Certainly I need your advice." She dropped her eyes. "If you would be so kind as to give it."

Guadalupita peered into the younger woman's face and then sat down again.

Alma frowned anxiously. "Kathy, what is it?"

Kathy took a deep, ragged breath. "I sent word to Peter that I am with child." She glanced up, then at the floor. "He is a good man. He will have to marry me now."

Alma's hand went to her mouth. "Oh, Kathy," she said. "Are you certain?"

Kathy looked up. A grim little smile passed over her pale face. "I'm certain that I sent him the message."

Guadalupita chuckled.

Alma shook her head. "I don't understand."

"After my foolishness last month, it's the only possible way to obtain his parents' agreement." Kathy turned her head, avoiding her friend's eyes. "And it will be true soon enough after we're married."

"Then you're not actually…"

"It's the only way I could think of."

"But surely they'll know that you aren't actually…"

Kathy shook her head. "It's too soon to tell without an physical examination." She turned to Guadalupita. "I am not Catholic. The priest is almost certain to ask for confirmation from a curandera."

"This Peter is the Taos joven? Oscar Lujan's younger son?" Guadalupita asked. "I think his mother will ask, if the priest does not. I have heard that she is very angry that you rejected her precious hijo."

"I was a fool." Kathy dropped her head. "I know that now." She looked up, her eyes pleading. "Señora Otero, would you confirm it for me?"

"And if you do not become pregnant immediately after el casamiento, the marriage?"

"I will say that I lost the child."

Guadalupita clicked her tongue and shook her head.

"And what about Peter?" Alma asked. "Will he believe you?"

Kathy smiled and her cheeks reddened. "He will know it is not true. We have never— I wouldn't let him—" She looked down at her hands, then took a deep breath and met Alma's eyes. "If he responds with a message acknowledging the child, I will know he has forgiven my foolishness. If he sends a message rejecting it, or if he doesn't respond, then I will try—" She bit her lip. "I will try to forget him," she whispered. She covered her face with her hands. "And I will never forgive myself," she sobbed.

"Oh, Kathy." Alma crossed the room to kneel beside Kathy's chair and put an arm around her friend's shoulders. "Are you certain this is the only way?"

Kathy took her hands from her face. "I can think of no other." She lifted her chin. "I don't know whether or not I have done the right thing, but that is what I have done. I won't go back now."

Guadalupita chuckled. "Verdad you are a child no longer, I think." She looked out the window for a long moment, then turned to the girl and gave a sharp little nod. "I will help you."

"Oh, señora," Kathy said. "I don't know how to thank you."

"You would perjure yourself?" Alma blurted in surprise.

The old lady compressed her lips. "I will help you." The girls stared at her determined eyes and knew that it was not for Kathy that she was doing this thing. But the look in Guadalupita's face did not invite questioning. "But for now, we will make soap," the curandera said firmly.

~ ~ ~ ~

As she made her slow way back to her family's campsite that afternoon, Guadalupita pondered her decision. It had been made on the spur of the moment, but it felt inevitable. Sixty-some years ago her mother had lain with a young Apache man. She herself was the result of that summer romance.

But her abuela, her mother's mother, was one who clung fiercely to the purity of her Spanish blood. She had rejected any possibility of marriage between the young people and badgered her daughter into a rapid casamiento with a pure-blooded widower who had three young sons, a temper, and a penchant for liquor. It was of no importance that he was a drunk and a wife beater. The unborn child would be baptized with a Spanish lineage.

Guadalupita hadn't known her true origins until she herself was married and her mother lay dying. Always she had wondered why her father and abuela disliked her so much. It had been a relief to discover that she was not related to the hombre who had caused her and her mamá so much pain.

She knew Peter's mother, of her pride in her Pueblo blood lines. Guadalupita shook her head. She would not stand by while another young woman lost her güiso, her sweetheart, as a result of such foolishness. There would be pain enough in the day-to-day living of their love, with a mother-in-law always looking to find fault.

The old curandera stopped to rest, eyes contemplating the green-black mountains that lined the western side of the valley. Below the opposite slopes lay the Taos Pueblo. Guadalupita shook her head and smiled, recalling the look in the blond girl's face as she'd said "That is what I have done. I won't go back now." She was a strong one, that Katarina. Stronger than she knew.

The old woman turned and began walking again. As for perjuring herself: Hah! She was not afraid of the priests. She had ceased listening to them seven years before, on that January morning in the American year 1847 when so many had died in the Taos revolt, including her own esposo. Those who inveigh against a thing and then are horrified when their listeners take action against the thing execrated deserve no respect. They do not speak for el dios.

Guadalupita's chin jerked defiantly upward, unconsciously mimicking the movement of Kathy's face three hours before.[16]

---

[16] Taos Pueblo lies about two miles northeast of the town of Don Fernando de Taos. Its first multi-story adobe buildings were constructed around AD 1350 and have been inhabited ever since. The Tiwa people who live there have a long and proud tradition. While New Mexico is remarkable for the way its three cultures (Native, Spanish, and Euroamerican) live together in relative peace, there have always been complications. This story acknowledges that young people can sometimes cross cultural lines more easily than adults, especially when love is involved.

The assistance the young people receive from Guadalupita is grounded in an instance when adaptation was enforced, rather than invited: the American response to the 1847 Taos Revolt. Her defiance of the Catholic priesthood is based on the idea, still held by some historians, that Taos' Catholic priest, Padre Martinez, incited the revolt, but then backpedaled when it failed.

TRAVELIN' MAN

Old One Eye Pete has been in the Pecos wilderness all winter, him and the mule, avoiding Apaches and harvesting beaver. The weather has been dry and mild for the most part, the resulting pelts poor to middling. But it's been a peaceful season over all and he's almost sorry when the first cottonwood buds start greening the trees.

He heads down slope then, and out onto the edge of the eastern plains. He works his way north along the base of the foothills, taking his time, moving from one greening meadow to the next, letting the mule feed, killing an antelope or small deer when he needs meat, and skirting the few settlements he comes upon.

He's in no hurry for human company just yet. The beaver plews aren't going to fetch much, no matter when he gets them to market. He can take his time.

But as he nears the Cimarron River, the usual dust-filled spring winds pick up and the mule objects vociferously to plodding through clouds of grit.

Old Pete chuckles in sympathy. Conditions like these almost make a man think four walls and a roof might not be such a bad thing.

Pete squints his good eye at the Cimarron. The river isn't quite as unruly as it usually is this time of year. He studies it for a long moment, then decides to follow the stream to its source and head on west from there to Taos.

By the end of the day, he's well inside the Cimarron's canyon. He makes camp at the base of a long sky-scraping cliff of jagged rock. The setting sun glints like gold on its crest.

Pete grunts. Maybe sights like this were what gave the Spanish the idea that this land held cities of gold. As far as Old Pete's concerned, with the sunlight on them like that, those towering cliffs are prettier than any gold.

He shakes his head at mankind's general greed and foolishness, and hobbles the mule. Then he sweeps leaf litter from the flat top of a knee-high granite boulder and builds a small fire.

He heats water and adds a quarter of his remaining coffee. As it steeps, he arranges small heaps of river rock alongside the fire, then cuts and trims a handful of green willow branches. He slices thin strips of meat from the remaining antelope haunch and weaves the strips onto the sticks, then wedges them between the rocks to angle the meat over the flames.

Old Pete sits back on his heels and reaches for the coffee. The brownish liquid isn't very tasty, but it's hot. He sips at it while he waits for the meat to sizzle.

He squints his good eye up at the cliffs, contemplating their grandeur again, then gazes toward the west. The sky is a clear bright blue above the mountains up canyon.

The mountains' bulk blocks the setting sun and the resulting shadows turn the slopes facing Pete into a solid black mass, making the sky above them even brighter. As he eats, the blue in the west becomes more and more luminous, then pales, darkens, and finally gives way to stars.

When he's finished his meal, Old Pete rolls himself into his blanket and sleeps. He keeps his rifle beside him, not because he feels in any danger but because it's the thing a man does when he's alone in the wilderness, a habit he formed long ago.

The next morning, man and mule mosey on up the canyon. They don't dally, but they don't hurry none, either. The sun glints on the stream, water striders dance across the water, and fish trace the striders. Old Pete contemplates the long narrow shapes of trout slipping through the shadowed pools and considers stopping to hook one, then decides to wait a mite longer.

He enters a small meadow. A clutch of wild turkeys move ahead of him, scratching along the base of the streamside willows. Pete grins at the way the birds pretend not to see him as they stay just out of reach. They're unusually plump and sleek for this time of year. With so little winter snow, they've had an easy time of it.

He moves on, like the turkeys seemingly in no hurry and unaware of his surroundings, but absorbing it all just the same. With the warming weather, the coyote willow beside the river has developed a haze of tiny green leaves that brightens the winter red of its bark. Under the tall green pines, waxy white flowers glow on sprigs of wild grape-holly. Sunlight filters through the long needles of the thick barked ponderosas and glints on the twisted branches of the scrub oaks below, still stubbornly bare.

In the late afternoon, Old Pete stops in a meadow to water and graze the mule while he gathers wild greens for his supper. He rinses them in a small creek that feeds into the Cimarron, then sits on a downed cottonwood log and nibbles contentedly on a handful of the sweet herbs. This is better than any so-called civilized garden. He'd just as soon stay out here forever, if he didn't need coffee.[17]

---

[17] The rock formation in the Cimarron River canyon that Old Pete admires so much is known today as the Palisades. This spectacular, vertically jointed rock cliff face is the geological highlight of the canyon, but one doesn't have to be a geologist to appreciate it, especially in the light of the setting sun.

THE NUEVOMEXICANO BOY

He was a well-mannered nuevomexicano boy and so he did not look directly into her face as he stood at the bottom of the wooden porch steps in his traditional loose cotton trousers and shirt. Alma took the opportunity to study him. He was perhaps twelve, on the brink of adolescence. He reminded her of her brother at that age: long limbs, a kind of tenderness about the mouth to which he would never admit, chest just beginning to expand into adult curves. Those muscles were bound to be larger by the end of the summer, if she chose to take him on for the haying. His own mother wouldn't recognize him when he returned home.

Alma had been sweeping the porch when the boy arrived and she resumed her work now, thinking it over. He said he knew how to hay, which was plausible, given his age and heritage. Her brother Andrew was in the fields below the hillside cabin, assessing the vega grass for its readiness. They could use another set of hands besides the three Anglo men camped behind the barn. Alma pursed her lips. How would the boy fare with the men they'd already hired?

Behind her, the cabin door opened. The boy's face sparked when he saw Ramón, the ranch cook and handyman. "Buenos días, señor," he said formally. "My father sends you his greetings."

The old man moved across the porch. "You are the son of my friend, Jésus Eduardo Garcia." It was a statement, the evidence of Ramón's remarkable ability to remember faces and body types. "You are his oldest?"

"Oh no, señor," the boy said. "That is José Eduardo. I am Juan Antonio, his third son." He smiled shyly. "And there is another after me, as well as two daughters."

"It has been a great while since I spoke with your father," Ramón said. "He is well?"

"Si, señor. He sent me to you—" The boy realized his mistake and glanced anxiously at Alma. "He sent me here to request work because he knew it was a good place."

Alma's lips twitched. "You would be working with men far older than you," she said. "Americano men. Your papá may not have been aware that this would be so."

The boy nodded, eyes again respectfully on the wooden steps. "He said it might be so." He glanced at the fields, where Andrew was now moving toward the house, then turned back to Alma. "He said the work is that of men and that you hire fairly."

The child will go far, Alma thought wryly. "All right," she said. "If my brother agrees."

~ ~ ~ ~

The change in government had brought many new things with it when nuevomexico became the United States' New Mexico Territory, but in the Moreno Valley there'd been few innovations and hay was still cut in the traditional way. Each morning, a line of men moved steadily across the broad dew-covered fields, long wooden-handled scythes whirring through the thick knee-high grass, which released a sweet green smell as it dropped. Blackbirds rose as the men approached, their red and yellow shoulder patches flashing in the sunlight.

From the cabin porch, Alma could see that the nuevomexicano boy clearly knew his business: his grasp firm on the scythe handle, feet apart, knees slightly bent, pivoting smoothly, at one with his scythe. When the morning's mowing was complete and the men began forming the newly cut grass into long narrow windrows, the boy handled the wooden-toothed hay rake as if he'd been born with it in his hands.

Alma watched for a long while before she finally stirred and went back inside to help Ramón set the table for the mid-day meal.

~ ~ ~ ~

Even with the cabin windows and doors open to the afternoon breeze, the house felt confined. Alma took her sewing to the heavy wooden bench on the porch. In the fields, the men were turning the windrows again, carefully flipping the cut hay to ensure that it dried evenly.

Her eyes skimmed over the Anglo men in their brown or blue breeches and high-smelling wool shirts, to the nuevomexicano boy in his traditional loose cotton. He hadn't succumbed to the need to dress like the Americans, she thought approvingly.

Or his parents hadn't, she corrected herself with a bemused smile. The clothes were clearly homemade. What would it be like to sew for a child of one's own? she wondered and was surprised at the twinge of envy she felt for the boy's mother. Alma shook her head. Such thoughts were sheer foolishness. To have a child, there must be a man, and she had no interest in marriage.

Or so she had thought. Her hands lay empty in her lap as she gazed unseeing at the mountains on the opposite side of the valley. After all, marriage was not just between a man and a woman. There was also the possibility of a child. Perhaps more than one. But marriage would almost certainly involve leaving the valley. Not even her brother found this long stretch of grass and timber between the Sangre de Cristo and Cimarron ranges as compelling a place to live as she did.

Besides, she was past thirty, too old to be thinking seriously about taking a husband, bearing a child. Alma gave her head a brisk shake and returned to her work.

PROTECTION

Samuel was playing near the edge of the forest while Gregoria knelt in the small garden. She glanced occasionally toward the log cabin at the other end of the clearing. Charles would return soon. The setting sun sent shadows across the grass. Samuel poked at the brown earth with a stick.

A cougar slunk forward between the scrub oak at the edge of the clearing and watched carefully, ears forward. Her tail twitched.

As the big cat positioned itself to spring, Gregoria's head snapped up. Her hand reached for a thick stick lying nearby. As the cat moved, so did she.

The woman was faster.

"No!" she shrieked as the mountain lion sprang toward the child. "No!" The stick flew through the air, hitting the cat's shoulder. The cougar arched away in mid-spring, missing its quarry. Samuel let out a cry, and the big cat snarled, then was gone.

"Mamá?" the child whimpered.

She reached for him wordlessly.

~ ~ ~ ~

When Charles came in from the mountainside pasture, mother and son were huddled on the cabin's only bed,

Gregoria curled around the child until he was almost invisible. She raised a tear-stained face.

Charles glanced at her and turned to hang his coat on a peg.

"Cuguar," she choked.

"Cougar?" Then he was beside her, pulling Samuel from her arms, looking him over.

"He is unhurt," she said, a hand on the child's small leg. "I threw a stick. It ran away."

Charles dumped him back into her arms. "Mountain lion don't run off." He crossed to the fire. "Don't tell me stories."

"It is true." Gregoria smoothed the boy's hair. "Mamá saved you," she told him. "She did."

Charles grunted at the fire. "You sittin' there with him all day?" he demanded. "Where's my food?"

She lowered the child gently to the bed and went to prepare the evening meal.

~ ~ ~ ~

"She threw a stick at a mountain cat that was goin' after the boy and it run off?" the old man who was visiting asked. "Mid-lunge?" The two men sat on stools in front of the cabin fire, a whisky jug between them.

"That's what she says."

They both turned to look at Gregoria, who sat on the bed in the corner, singing a lullaby to the child, crooning him to sleep.

"Hard to believe," the old man said, stroking his stringy white beard.

"Old cat," Charles said.

"Maybe." The old man took a sip from the jug. "Coulda been a young one, though. A woman's protective instincts can be almighty strong."

There was a disbelieving grunt at the fire and then silence.

"Stranger things've happened," the old man observed. "And she does take kindly to that child."

"She does that," her husband said grudgingly.[18]

---

[18] This story is based on an incident that occurs in the novel *The Pain and The Sorrow,* Sunstone Press, 2017. Set in the late 1860s and reflecting actual characters and events, *The Pain and The Sorrow* is about Gregoria's realization that her abusive husband is also a serial killer and what happens when she finally takes action.

BUZZARD BRAINS

"He ain't got the brains God gave a buzzard," the old man grumbled. He picked up his mattock and glared at the black-hatted figure retreating down the bottom of Humbug Gulch toward Elizabethtown.

Then he looked uphill, toward Baldy Peak. "Idiot can't even figure out there's a storm up there and this gully likely t' wash out in another half hour." He sniffed disdainfully and went back to work, breaking rock on the gully's southern lip, searching for the gold that was bound to be there if a man worked the stones long enough.

The young man in the black bowler hat chewed thoughtfully on his lower lip as he trudged down the center of the gulch through the gravel and broken rock. He'd offered every dollar he had for the claim, but the miner clearly wasn't interested in selling. He shook his head. There must be other options.

Halfway down the slope, he paused to catch his breath and gaze at the mountain above. That dark cloud spoke rain. Given the southeast position of the cloud and the angle of Humbug Gulch, it was unlikely that particular cloudburst would wet this particular gully. However, just to be on the safe side, he moved halfway up the gully's north slope before he continued his downward trek.

The sun was glaringly bright on the dry rocks. The young man sat down on a sandstone boulder and took off his hat. He brushed at the dust on the black felt and shook his head. He needed to find something lighter weight and less apt to show dust. He'd keep wearing this in the meantime, though. If nothing else, it protected him from sunstroke.

He glanced down at the shadowed side of his rocky seat and grinned. Like this boulder was protecting that bit of grass, growing here among the pitiless rocks where no plant had a right to be.

The young man's eyes narrowed and he leaned forward. He shaded the clump of grass with his hat and peered down at it and the rocks around it.

Then he straightened abruptly, glanced up the gully where the miner had gone back to work, and slid off the boulder. He crouched beside the big rock and gently pried a piece of broken quartz from the ground. He turned it slowly back and forth, examining every facet and seam.

Five minutes later, the young man sat back on his heels and turned the rock again, just to be certain. Then he picked up a stick and poked around a bit in the ground beside the boulder.

He nodded thoughtfully, then stood and looked carefully at the gulch's rocky slopes for any sign of possession. But this piece of land clearly hadn't been claimed. Apparently, no one had thought there was gold this far down Humbug Gulch.

The young man chuckled, tucked the piece of quartz into his pocket, clapped his dusty black hat on his head, and headed into Elizabethtown to file the necessary paperwork for his claim.[19]

---

[19] Humbug Gulch is located on the western slope of Baldy Mountain, directly across from the mining camp of Elizabethtown in New Mexico's Sangre de Cristos.

A Poor Laborin' Man

John Gallagher stops at the dusty corner of Washington and First and stares at the gangly wooden structure that sprawls across the mountain slope opposite Elizabethtown. Then he turns and accosts the first man who glances at him. Gallagher waves his hand at the mountainside. "If you would be tellin' me, good sir, if it please you, what would you be callin' that monstrosity yonder?"

The old man peers at Gallagher with his one good eye, then looks at the mountain and scratches thoughtfully at his scraggly white beard. He chuckles. "Well, some of us are callin' it Maxwell's Folly. Lucien Maxwell himself is callin' it the Big Ditch."

He pushes his battered broad-brimmed felt hat back from his forehead. "And then others are callin' it an engineer's dream." He grins at the younger man. "Dream like a fantasy."

"Fantastical it most certainly seems," Gallagher agrees. "It puts me in mind of a centipede on tall legs." He shakes his head. "It's three years I've been travellin' this country and 'tis the first of its kind I've had the pleasure of viewin'."

"You Irish?" the other man asks.

Gallagher grins. "And what was it caused you to be thinkin' such a thing?"

The old man chuckles. Together they contemplate the tall wooden structure that runs along the side of the mountain and the small figures that clamber up and around it.

"But what is the thing's purpose?" the Irishman asks. "If I may be so bold as to ask."

"Well now, the West Point engineer who designed it says the trough at the top is gonna carry water from the mountain lakes west of here." The old man waves towards the pine and fir covered slopes behind them. Then he points across the narrow valley at their feet to a stone-filled gulch that runs straight down the mountain opposite and ends just below the town.

"Baldy Mountain's slopes are full of rocks and some of 'em contain good size pieces of gold," he says. "That engineer's got his investors convinced the miners'll want to wash the rock out and get at the gold more easy like." He shrugs. "Sounds reasonable enough. He's got some big backers. Not just Lucien Maxwell, who owns most of the land hereabouts, but V. S. Shelby, the man runnin' the stage you came in on." He glances at Gallagher. "If you came by way of Cimarron, which most newcomers do."

Gallagher nods. "Cimarron it was, but 'twas no stage for the likes of me." He spreads his big hands, palms up. "I'm a poor laborin' man with a sweetheart to bring over from the old country, soon as may be. That stage fare seemed a mite high for my tastes, so it was by walkin' that I arrived in this good mountain town." He shakes his head, as if remembering his journey, and clicks his tongue against his teeth. "Tis a grand and rugged country."

The old man looks at him with respect mingled with compassion. "That's quite a hike, Cimarron to here. And even men on foot still have to pay the road toll."

Gallagher grins. "It's ingenious I've been since I was a lad," he says. "And quick to find a way around payin' when it's not rightly needful."

"You went through the hills, huh? That's some rough going." The other man shakes his head as he studies the mountain opposite. "And they say the Irish are shiftless."

Gallagher's jaw tightens and his fists clench. "Who says it?"

The old man gives him a startled look. "Not me!" He puts up a hand. "Not me! No, sir!" He waits until the other man's fists unclench, then turns and gestures toward the wooden structure across the valley. "You know, if you're not lookin' to start mining right off, they're hirin' laborers," he says.

"And it's thankin' you I am for the suggestion," John Gallagher says stiffly.

"You tell 'em Old One Eye Pete sent ya." The old man reaches to slap Gallagher on the back, then seems to think better of it. He settles his battered hat back onto his forehead, gives Gallagher a nod, and heads down the street.

The Irishman nods after him, then turns his gaze back to the Big Ditch. Water from the mountain lakes westward, is it now? He runs his eyes over the sparse grass that dots Baldy Mountain's slopes, the richer green in the narrow valley below. Yes, water would be of some importance in this dry land. And the bringing of it a cause for concern.

And a sure source of income for the likes of him. He grins, thinking of the one hundred fifteen dollars in his money belt, waiting to be added to. Waiting to bring his Mary to this good land, to buy acreage, and raise children. Then he looks down at his hands, flexes them thoughtfully, and starts down the hill toward the structure they call Maxwell's Folly.[20]

---

[20] The Big Ditch, designed by Capt. Nicholas S. Davis, was a 40-plus mile water system that ran from the headwaters of New Mexico's Red River to the western slopes of Baldy Mountain, east of Elizabethtown. The flumes rested on a wooden structure that looked from a distance much like a giant centipede. The goal was to provide a steady water supply for hydraulic mining, but seepage and other issues resulted in significantly less water than expected.

The 1870 Census record for Elizabethtown lists John Gallagher as a 30-year-old laborer from Ireland. Although there's no evidence that he worked on the Big Ditch, it's certainly plausible.

Gallagher did well for himself in the Moreno Valley. By 1880, he was a married miner with three sons. A few years later, he owned land near what is today Eagle Nest Lake Dam and had begun constructing a two mile long irrigation ditch to carry water from Willow Creek to his fields there. By 1900, he was irrigating at least 140 acres and owned a great deal more land across the Valley.

DANGER SIGNS

"I sure could do with some raised biscuits," Peter Kinsinger said over his shoulder as he and his brother Joseph trudged east through the snow toward the top of Palo Flechado Pass.

He hitched the aspen pole that supported the yearling elk carcass between them into a more comfortable spot on his shoulder. "I hear tell Kennedy's wife knows how to make 'em real good. His place is only a few miles now and his prices are reasonable."

"You could wait for Elmira's biscuits," Joseph said. "She'll be waitin' on us." He hadn't liked the looks of the Kennedy cabin when they'd passed it on their way into the Pass and Taos Canyon beyond. They now had the meat they'd been hunting and he was tired of November snow and cold.

Peter turned his head and grinned. "I'm a mite chilly, ain't you? And thirsty. A fire and a little liquid refreshment would be a right comfort just about now."

Joseph chuckled. Peter's Elmira was a stickler about alcohol. Peter found it easier to stay away from the Elizabethtown saloons than to experience her tongue when he stumbled home from them.

But a man deserved a nip now and then. And with the weather so inclement, it was unlikely there'd be anyone else drinking the liquor or eating the meals that Kennedy sold to passersby.

"It is mighty cold out here," he acknowledged. "And we're still a good ways from home."

The road leveled out at the top of the Pass, then the brothers began to descend, careful of the icy patches in the shady spots. They were about a quarter of the way down the mountain when they heard the echo of first one rifle shot, then another.

"Sounds like Kennedy's huntin' too," Peter said.

"You may not get that drink after all," Joseph said. "I hear tell his woman don't open that cabin door if he ain't there."

"Too bad," Peter said. "I truly am thirsty."

Joseph chuckled. "It's still a ways. Maybe he'll be back before we get there."

But when they came within sight of the Kennedy place three-quarters of an hour later, they both forgot all about liquid refreshments.

A man lay face down in the middle of the frozen dirt track that skirted the Kennedy hollow. The snow and dirt were splashed red with blood. Charles Kennedy's bear-like form crouched beside the sprawled body.

The Kinsinger brothers eased their elk to the side of the road and hurried forward.

Kennedy looked up, his black beard bristling around a perpetually angry mouth, his eyes watchful. "Injuns," he said.

Peter and Joseph looked at each other, then Kennedy.

"Is he dead?" Peter asked.

Kennedy nodded. "I fought the Injuns off." He stood and gestured toward the cabin. "Bullet holes in th' door." He nudged the dead man's torso with the side of his boot. "Greenhorn ran."

Joseph leaned down, reached for the man's shoulder, and rolled him over. "I don't recognize him."

"Came from Taos," Kennedy said. "Merchant there. So he said."

Joseph straightened and looked away, down the road to Elizabethtown.

"When'd it happen?" Peter asked.

"Couple hours ago," Kennedy said.

The Kinsingers nodded, eyes raking the hollow and bloody snow, careful not to look at each other or Charles Kennedy.

"Well, we have meat to get home," Joseph said. "We'll tell the Sheriff's deputy in Etown, and he can come fetch the body." He looked down. "Whoever he is, I expect his Taos friends'll be wantin' to give him a proper burial."

Kennedy nodded. He stood next to the dead man and raked his fingers through his beard as the Kinsingers returned to their elk, hoisted its carrying pole onto their shoulders, and trudged past him.

The brothers were out of sight over the rise to the northeast before either of them spoke.

"Injuns my hat," Peter said over his shoulder.

Joseph spat into the snow at the side of the road. "Sure a convenient excuse though, ain't they?"

"We didn't see anything different," Peter pointed out.

"Wouldn't want to get crosswise of that one," Joseph agreed.

They trudged morosely on up the valley toward Elizabethtown.[21]

---

[21] This story is a revised extract from the novel *The Pain and The Sorrow*, Sunstone Press, 2017. It's based on an incident Joseph Kinsinger described in an 1885 interview for the *Silver City Sentinel*. In 1868, Ohio-born Joseph Kinsinger was about 33 and working as a laborer at the Etown Quartz Mill and Lode Company along with his 37-year-old brother Peter, a cooper. Joseph and Peter were both veterans of the Civil War and married—Joseph to Desideria Baca, with whom he had a daughter, and Peter to Ohio native Elmira. There's reason to believe that the Kinsingers were first on the scene of this particular death, since the *Sentinel* article provides details about it that aren't available from other sources.

ETOWN EXPERIENCE

She'd only been able to catch glimpses of the scenery as they'd travelled through the Cimarron River Canyon, but when Eliza stepped down from the Moreno Valley stagecoach, she saw that she was now truly in the mountains. She breathed a sigh of relief.

"Mademoiselle? May I assist you?" There was a Continental lilt to the man's voice.

She smiled at him gratefully. "I am looking for Mr. Henri Lambert," she said. "He is married to my good friend Mary."

"You must be Miss Dawkins!" the man said. "I am Henri Lambert. Mollie will be so pleased that you have arrived. Welcome to Elizabethtown, New Mexico Territory!"

He said it with such pride, she thought with amusement. As if he'd built the place himself. She examined the street and its people as she followed him and her trunk. It was a ramshackle, bustling kind of town. She liked it.

~ ~ ~ ~

"After the Great Rebellion, I just wanted to leave Virginia," Mary confided. She prowled restlessly around the room, touching the ornaments on the shelves and mantelpiece. "Henri was so travelled and so French. It was a pleasure to talk with a man who knew something of life besides battle and war." She turned to her friend. "We went to Denver first. It was rough, but it did have some culture." She raised both hands, palms up, then dropped them helplessly. "But there was little opportunity for another hotel and restaurant. When Henri heard about Elizabethtown, he was eager to come here."

"But you don't like it," Eliza said.

Mary frowned. "It doesn't agree with me," she said. "I cannot adjust to these altitudes and the chill. I long for warm southern nights."

Eliza chuckled. "Yes, I had noticed that the nights here are somewhat cooler than those of our childhood."

~ ~ ~ ~

Eliza paused to stare at the wooden structure that stretched down the valley like a great long-legged wooden centipede.

"What is it?" she wondered aloud.

A passing miner stopped, as if glad of an excuse to talk. "It's a flume, Ma'am," he said. "It's supposed to bring water from the Red River down this way, so we can wash the gold outta the hillsides."

She glanced at him. "You said 'supposed to.' Did it not work correctly?"

"Not enough, ma'am," he said. "They call it Davis's Folly, for the man that thought it up. Most of the water seeped out before it got here." He peered into her face. "You Molly Lambert's friend?"

Eliza frowned, but he grinned at her companionably. "Don't take offense, ma'am. A new face in Etown's bound to draw some attention." He pulled off his hat, as if suddenly aware of it. "I hope you're planning to stay a while, ma'am."

~ ~ ~ ~

"You went out alone?" Mary moved nervously around her small parlor.

"I was always in sight of the town," Eliza said. "I couldn't disappear without somebody noticing."

"Men have disappeared between here and Taos," Mary said grimly. "That Kennedy man was killing them."

"I wasn't going to Taos."

"I'm glad of that."

"I like it here," Eliza said. "The openness, the freedom."

"Then you will stay?"

"If I can find something to do. My savings are almost depleted."

Mary chuckled. "You'll be married within three months," she predicted. "If that's what you want."

Eliza laughed. "There do seem to be plenty of available men," she agreed. "But I'm not at all sure that's what I want."

Mary sat down. "No?"

"Men die so easily," Eliza said quietly, looking at her hands. "The war taught me that."

"Yes," Mary agreed softly. "It shadows us women as well as the men."

~ ~ ~ ~

"Henri has decided to sell the hotel and move to Cimarron," Mary said. "Business is slowing here, and the doctor says Cimarron's lower elevation and warmer temperatures may be better for my health."

Eliza put her teacup on the small parlor table. "I will miss you."

"It's not so very far. Only a short stage ride."

Eliza smiled. "It will be a little farther. I expect to be in Las Vegas."

Mary's teacup stopped halfway to her lips. "Las Vegas? I thought you didn't want to marry."

Eliza put her hands in her lap and looked down at them. "Charles Ilfeld has offered me a position as dry goods clerk."

"At his mercantile? But standing behind a counter all day…"

Eliza smiled. "I don't expect to clerk for very long. I'm beginning to think my aversion to matrimony is shortsighted."

Mary laughed and lifted her cup. "You should have plenty of opportunities there," she observed.

~ ~ ~ ~

Eliza pushed the curtain back from the open window, allowing more air into the room. It was almost as hot outside as in, but the slight draft helped a little. She stared into the dark street. In the bed behind her, Arthur moved restlessly. In the room down the uncarpeted hall, a child whimpered in his sleep.

Las Vegas could be so hot during the summer. She leaned her forehead against the window sash, thinking of the first New Mexican town she had lived in.

She missed Elizabethtown. She loved her husband and her children, but there were times when she longed for those rustic log buildings with the bark still clinging to the outside, Baldy Mountain looming above them to the east. The soft banks of Moreno Creek in the spring. Moreno River, she corrected herself with a smile.

"Eliza?" Arthur asked.

"Mama?" a small boy called.

She turned toward them.

~ ~ ~ ~

"It seems smaller," his mother said.

"It was twenty-five years ago," Arthur Jr. said. He lifted her carefully from the stagecoach into the dirt street outside the Mutz Hotel.

"I was bigger then, too," Eliza said ruefully. "With better eyesight." She turned her face to the east. "But I can still see Baldy Mountain."

"Does the air feel the same?"

She stood still, feeling the cool breeze. She nodded, then sniffed. "It smells the same, too." She smiled. "Dirt, animals, liquor, and men."

He chuckled. "Those are good smells?"

"In this clear air, yes." She paused. "It sounds different though. Quieter, somehow. Less hopeful."

"They're still working the gold. Working it again, I should say."

She shook her head. "It isn't the same, though." She sighed. "Nothing stays the same, does it? Everything changes."

He smiled down at her. "Except your good heart."

She patted his arm. "Let's go inside."[22]

---

[22] Although Eliza Dawkins and her family are fictional characters, the Lamberts are not. Henri Lambert was a Frenchman who worked as a cook for General U. S. Grant during the American Civil War and, in that capacity, served President Lincoln as well. In early 1868, Lambert married Mary 'Molly' Stepp of Petersburg, Virginia. They and her younger brother moved to Denver, and then to Elizabethtown, where Henri successfully operated a hotel and restaurant/saloon. In 1872, they moved to Cimarron and Henri established the hotel and saloon that operates today as the St. James Hotel and Restaurant.

When Molly mentions Charles Kennedy, she's referring to the serial killer who appears in "Protection" and "Danger Signs" and was lynched in Etown in Fall 1870. For a fictional account of Kennedy and the teenage wife who's report on his activities led to his death, see *The Pain and The Sorrow,* Sunstone Press, 2017.

The Las Vegas store where Eliza gets a job, Charles Ilfeld Company, was the largest mercantile firm in New Mexico Territory in the late 1800s. Headquartered in Las Vegas, it had branches throughout the Territory and sold everything from fashionable millinery to country produce.

When Eliza calls the stream below Elizabethtown 'Moreno Creek,' instead of 'Moreno River,' she's reflecting a change in nomenclature that seems to have occurred sometime during the late 1800s. The stream must have been flowing year-round in the 1860s, when it's routinely referred to as a river. Later in the century, unless the speaker was being facetious, it was usually called Moreno Creek.

Maxwell Before The Bar

Lucien Bonaparte Maxwell sits on one of the mismatched chairs in Elizabethtown's makeshift Colfax County courtroom and studies the man behind the judge's table. He's sat at such tables himself, though he doubts he ever looked so uncomfortable. Joseph Palen looks out of place here in this rough mining town and angry that it has the audacity to call itself a county seat. He apparently disapproves of nuevomexico, too, for that matter.

Maxwell feels the impulse to laugh, but instead lifts his right foot to his left knee and watches the crowd gather. Most of the men nod to him politely, touching their foreheads in a kind of salute, and he nods back. They're good people. Know what they want, have no pretense about them. He grins at Old Pete, who's still wearing his hat, even inside the courtroom.

Beside him, the old attorney Theodore Wheaton mutters, "Here we go," and Judge Palen gavels the room to attention.

"Apparently, Mr. Maxwell has deigned to honor us with his presence this morning," Palen says, glaring at Lucien.

Maxwell resists the impulse to straighten his spine and put both feet on the floor. "I believe you wanted to see me," he says coolly.

Judge Palen's lips tighten. "You have an interest in a number of cases before this court."

Maxwell nods and tilts his head toward the old lawyer beside him. "Mr. Wheaton is my designated attorney," he says. "I believe that releases me from the need to be present." He adjusts his right foot higher on his left knee.

"You have also been indicted on a serious charge." Palen leans forward. "That indictment requires your attendance."

"The probate court issue?" Maxwell lifts a shoulder. "We have an excellent probate court clerk. As you'll see from his records, there was no need to hold formal court."

Palen's lips thin. "You committed to appearing on the first day of this session in regard to the indictment against you. It is now the fourth day."

"I was unexpectedly detained."

Palen stares at him for a long moment, then turns to the court clerk. "Let the record show that Mr. Maxwell has appeared and apologized for his failure to appear, and that we are satisfied no contempt was intended."

Maxwell's jaw tightens, then he nods slightly and pulls his right foot more firmly onto his knee. If that's the way the man wants to play it, he can adjust.

~ ~ ~ ~

"Things are changing, Mr. Maxwell." Judge Joseph Palen sets his whisky glass on the saloon table and looks around the room. "In another year or so, these ragged placer miners will be replaced by businessmen with laborers to do the rough work."

Maxwell nods, following his gaze. "And many of these men will be laborers, instead of independent men with claims of their own," he says ruefully.

"Claims so poorly worked they bring in barely enough to keep body and soul together." Palen flicks a speck of dust from the sleeve of his dark broadcloth suit.

"That's all that matters, I suppose." Maxwell grimaces. "Efficiency."

"It's a large territory, and its resources are going to waste."

"So they tell me," Maxwell says. He shakes his head, puts his glass on the table, and reaches for his battered black hat. "I've been here a long time, Mr. Palen, and I happen to like nuevomexico's lack of efficiency. So do most of the men in this room, I expect. Though none of us are averse to making a penny or two." He stands, towering over the table. "Good day to you, Judge." A mischievous smile flashes across his face. "And good luck."[23]

---

[23] This story is based on events that occurred during the Spring 1870 First Judicial District Court session in Elizabethtown, the Colfax County seat. Lucien Maxwell, as Colfax County Probate Judge, was indicted for not holding court, but the charges were dismissed.

At the time, Maxwell and his wife were in the final stages of selling the Beaubien/Miranda Land Grant (aka the Maxwell Land Grant) to a consortium of English investors. Judge Joseph Palen was newly appointed to his position as Justice for the First District Court of New Mexico. He would go on to become an important member of the notorious Santa Fe Ring, which sought to monetize the agricultural and other assets of New Mexico Territory.

BROTHERLY LOVE

Herman bent carefully over the precious paper. "Dear Gertrude," he wrote in German. "Pete and me are in Elizabethtown, New Mexico Territory. We are cutting timbers for the miners and making good money. I have enough for land and a house. The grass is good and summers are pleasant. I am sending the money for your passage. Please come soon."

The young woman in the tiny Austrian village who received this letter considered it thoughtfully. She wasn't sure she loved this man. His brother was more pleasant to talk to. But marrying Herman meant she could leave poverty behind.

Gertrude began her preparations, then wrote her own letter. "Dear Herman," it said. "I begin my journey in twelve days. My uncle says travel on the railroad to Denver, then send for you to collect me. I will write again when I arrive."

Herman's heart sang with joy when he read these words.

~ ~ ~ ~

When Peter entered the small log cabin he shared with his brother in Elizabethtown, Herman was washing dishes. "I got a message," Herman said abruptly. "Gertrude, she is in Denver."

"That's good!" Peter said heartily.

Herman shook his head anxiously. "I am not ready," he said. "The house, it is not finished, and this cabin is not fit for a woman."

Peter shrugged. "She will make it right, the way she wants it."

Herman shook his head. "It should be right for her," he insisted. "I am not ready."

Peter turned away.

"Will you go for her while I make it ready?" Herman asked.

Peter paused, staring at the wall of roughly caulked logs. "I suppose that would be possible," he said slowly. He turned to face his brother. "I can start in two days."

Herman smiled in relief. "Thank you!" he said gratefully. "I thank you!"

Peter nodded unhappily.

~ ~ ~ ~

Herman waited anxiously for his bride and his brother to arrive in Elizabethtown from Denver. After two weeks went by, he began to worry. Was Gertrude sick? Had an accident befallen Peter on his way to collect her?

Then a letter arrived. The messenger delivered it while Herman was drinking at the bar in Herberger's Saloon. He tore it open and began to read, then groped blindly for a chair. He read it again. The men around him fell silent as Herman's face grew paler.

"Your bride take sick?" the bartender asked. "Or Pete?"

Herman passed his hand over his face, then looked around.

"He married her," he said. "They're coming back now."

Someone started to laugh, then stopped abruptly.

Herman got up and walked to the door. Then he turned. "I'll be in my new house," he said. "Tell Peter and Gertrude they can—" He shook his head. "Have the cabin."

~ ~ ~ ~

"Here's the sugar and the coffee," Pauli said as he entered the tiny log house.

His mother was sitting by the fire nursing the baby. "Danke," she said, smiling at him. The English he spoke so easily was still difficult for her, even after eight years in New Mexico Territory.

"Mr. Pearson asked me how my Uncle Herman was getting along," Pauli said. "Does he mean old Herman the miner?"

His mother gave him a puzzled frown, and he repeated his question in German. The door behind him opened as he spoke.

His father came in with an armful of firewood, and boy and woman looked up at him.

"He is my brother," Pauli's father said stiffly. "He don't talk to us."

"Why, papa?"

His parents exchanged glances.

"He don't, is all," his father said. He turned to the woman. "Is this enough firewood for the dinner?"

~ ~ ~ ~

Pauli had never seen his father Peter weep. The man had been grief-stricken but tearless when Pauli's mother died. It had been expected, and there was relief that her pain was over.

Now, the twenty-year-old sat at the old wooden table in the tiny log cabin and felt the older man's hands tremble in his. "My brother is dead," his father muttered. He nodded at the piece of paper on the table between them. "Herman is dead."

Pauli released his father's hand and reached for the paper. It was a will, in English, signed and witnessed. He squinted in the poor light. It left the house and three Elizabethtown District mining claims to Peter, then to Pauli and his sister after Peter's death. At the bottom of the paper were two sentences, scrawled in German. "I understand," they said. "She was a good woman."

Pauli's father covered his face and wept.[24]

---

[24] In the summer of 1870, when this story begins, Etown's citizens included emigrants from the German States, Austria, Canada, England, Mexico, Italy, Russia, Switzerland, Scandinavia, and Tunisia, as well as various parts of the United States and its territories. While many of these men would marry women from New Mexico, it was not uncommon for immigrant men to scrape together the funds to pay for passage for a sweetheart from home. But there was no guarantee she would marry the man who'd sent the money in question.

AMBITIONS

"Where'd you be gettin' a name like Leonidas?" the young Irishman asked the tall young man next to him at the Elizabethtown bar.

The big Canadian looked at him. "My mother had scholarly ambitions beyond her station," he said. He lifted a fist. "Although my father made sure I could defend myself."

"I'd not be denying you the right to the name." George Cunningham grinned. "And I'm thinking your father trained you good and well."

"The trouble is, they didn't have the money for proper scholarship," Leonidas Van Valser said ruefully. He lifted his glass toward the door. "That's why I'm here."

"Get enough gold, you won't be having to worry about scholarship," Cunningham observed.

"I intend to pan enough gold to go to school properly," Van Valser explained. "I'm only twenty-five. There's still time."

"You've got ambitions," Cunningham said. "'Tis a good thing in a man."

The two grinned at each other companionably.

~ ~ ~ ~

George Cunningham was small, even for an Irishman, with a perpetually restless face. His Canadian friend

Leonidas Van Valser was the steady one, until Etown's gold placer mines wore down even his perseverance.

"There must be an easier way to make a living," Leonidas said one night in Herberger's saloon as he examined his bandaged hand. He'd had a run-in that morning with some unstable sandstone.

"Somewhere else, is what I've been thinking," Cunningham said. "Anywhere but these water-forsaken rock-bound hills."

Van Valser nodded gloomily. "I think you've finally convinced me, George. But I don't know what to do about it."

"It's cattle I've been thinking of."

"Neither of us have cattle."

"There's plenty of cattle roamin' these hills with nary a brand mark to be seen."

"That's rustling," Leonidas said.

"Not if you don't get yourself caught." Cunningham bent toward him.

Van Valser studied his friend's face. "I'm listening," he said.

~ ~ ~ ~

"Do you know anything about cows?" Leonidas asked as he studied the longhorns in the clearing below.

"Aye, I was in Texas for a while after the war," Cunningham said. "Though my size was against me, I do admit." The little Irishman grinned at his friend. "But you've got the leverage to bring those yearlings onto their sides smooth as Irish whisky." He hefted the rope in his hand. "I rope 'em, you flip 'em, then we brand and sell 'em to the first Etown slaughterhouse we come to."

"It's certainly worth a try," Leonidas agreed. "Beef's selling at a good price and the slaughterhouses aren't too careful about ownership, from what I hear." He looked at the herd. "Who do they actually belong to?"

Cunningham shrugged. "Some Texan turned 'em loose on grass that don't belong to him. To my mind, we're just helping the Maxwell Company even the score."

~ ~ ~ ~

"You git off my property!" The woman was thin as a garter snake, with the eyes of a rattler. She glared at the two dusty young men down the cold steel of a rifle barrel. "And git your hands up!"

Van Valser and Cunningham did as she said, their horses shifting beneath them.

"We do apologize, ma'am," Cunningham said. "We were hoping for a wee bit of water from your well. Driving cattle is hard work on such an uncommonly warm day as it is."

She studied them. Her mouth twitched as she looked at Van Valser, whose face was streaked with dusty sweat. She lowered her rifle and gestured toward the well. "Help yourself," she said. "But only to the water. Not my cattle or anything else. Then git on outta here before you get caught."

"Yes, ma'am," they said in unison.

"Godforsaken young idiots," she muttered as she watched them dismount.

~ ~ ~ ~

George was getting nervous. "Let's get ourselves off this main track," he said. "These cattle are making our trail a wee bit too readable."

Leonidas nodded. "We can head up Ute Creek," he suggested. "Maybe offer them for sale at Baldy Camp instead of driving them clear to Etown."

The longhorns moved gladly into the Ute Creek grasslands, but then stalled. The forage was long and green, and they saw no reason to go on. George whooped and waved his hat at them half-heartedly. He was losing enthusiasm for this whole venture. His pony wasn't really a cow horse and didn't care for close proximity to longhorns. And he liked Leonidas, but the big Canadian hadn't adapted to cowherding as easily as he'd hoped. He sighed. Etown placer mining, and now this. He should just head on back to Ireland.

Leonidas rode up beside him. "How much farther?" he asked.

~ ~ ~ ~

Tom Stockton pushed back his hat and wiped his forehead with his shirt sleeve. Even the rippling sound of the nearby Cimarron river did nothing to relieve the heat.

Chuck, Finis, and the others reined in on either side of him. They all stared at the hoof marks on the rocky dirt road heading into Cimarron canyon.

"They ain't even trying to cover their tracks or keep those cattle where it won't show," Finis said with disgust.

~ ~ ~ ~

As the cluster of men and cattle entered the east end of the canyon, George Cunningham's hopes revived. Tom Stockton had his longhorns back, and he and his men were paying more attention to the cattle than to Cunningham and Van Valser. There'd been no move to string them up.

The green farmlands east of Cimarron Canyon were almost within sight. George began looking carefully at the sandstone and juniper on either side of the road. It might just be possible to make a dash for it. He glanced around. Van Valser was behind him. George slowed his pony a little to angle closer, letting the cattle ease by.

But Stockton had seen him examining the landscape, and suddenly Chuck and Finis were riding toward the two rustlers. There was a sudden blast of gunfire. Cunningham's pony reared, Leonidas crumpled in his saddle, and everything went black.

"Trying to escape," Tom Stockton growled. "The damn fools."[25]

---

[25] This story is based on an incident reported in Michael R. Maddox's *Porter and Ike Stockton, Colorado and New Mexico Border Outlaws.* The Company referred to here is the Maxwell Land Grant and Railway Company, the group of investors to whom Lucien and Luz Maxwell had sold the Maxwell Land Grant two years earlier.

The Company was working hard at this point to clear the grant of unauthorized 'squatters,' including miners and ranchers, but it's doubtful they were concerned about Thomas Stockton's cattle. Stockton, as part owner of the Clifton House on the Santa Fe Trail, a way station for cattle drives, had a certain standing in the community. At the inquest into Cunningham and Van Valser's death, his actions were deemed justifiable homicide, since the two men had been escaping when they were shot.

THE POLLOCK FAMILY'S NAVAJO BOY

Sarah was only sixteen when she married Thomas Pollock and she's never been sorry, but there are times when she wonders if they're both crazy. Especially now, as he sits across from her at the rough-hewn wooden table in their Colorado miner's cabin and jiggles two-year-old Charlie on his knee.

"What do you think?" he asks the child. "Shall we find our fortune in New Mexico Territory?"

Sarah shakes her head and lifts baby Josephine to her shoulder to burp. Six-year-old Jessie appears at her elbow, slate in hand. Sarah glances at it. "'Territory' is spelled wrong," she says. Jessie flashes her a smile and retreats and Sarah grins wryly. "I think I've just been outvoted," she tells Thomas. "When do you want to leave?"

Thomas stands up and tosses Charlie into the air. The little boy squeals in delight.

"Gonna be rich!" Thomas exults.

"Going to be together, anyway," Sarah says.

~ ~ ~ ~

New Mexico Territory is drier than Colorado, but not much different otherwise, Thomas reflects as the covered wagon rattles south out of Raton Pass. He clucks at the mules, who twitch their ears and keep steadily on. The three children are asleep in the back of the wagon and

Sarah has slipped down to gather wildflowers. The wagon rolls steadily across the plains.

Thomas yawns. He spent his boyhood in Ohio farmland, and that was enough grassland for him. He'll be glad to get to Elizabethtown and back in the mountains. And working again, instead of clucking at mules all day long.

There's a light thump behind him. Thomas turns his head. Jessie smiles at him sleepily. "How much farther, papa?" she asks.

"As far as we can get," he answers with a grin. He clucks at the mules again. They twitch their ears and keep steadily on.

~ ~ ~ ~

Finally, they're heading into mountains again. "This road needs some improvement," Sarah observes as the wagon jolts up Cimarron Canyon. Her arms tighten around baby Josephine.

"It does that," Thomas agrees.

Among the goods in the wagon bed, Charlie begins to cry. "I bumped my head!" he howls.

"You better be quiet, or the Indians'll get us!" his older sister says.

Sarah and Thomas look at each other.

"Well, there are Indians," Sarah points out. They'd seen them at Maxwell's Ranch, standing in silent groups outside the grist mill, waiting for their dole of grain.

"And soldiers," Thomas reminds her.

Sarah looks up at the sandstone cliffs on either side of the rocky track and shivers. "I'll be glad when we get to Elizabethtown," she says.

"I don't know how much of a town it'll be," Thomas warns.

"Anything will be better than this wilderness," she answers.

~ ~ ~ ~

They stop for the night at a spot where the canyon widens slightly. The Cimarron River is slower here, beaver dams backing it into a series of pools. Thomas fashions poles so he and Jessie can fish.

"You're too little to come. You'll scare the fish," Jessie tells Charlie loftily as they leave the campsite.

The little boy pouts for a minute, then settles to playing with some glittery rocks. Meanwhile, Sarah builds a fire, slices bacon into a cast iron skillet to render fat for the trout, then goes to the back of the wagon to nurse the baby. She's buttoning her chemise when she hears a clatter. Charlie cries out.

As Sarah darts around the end of the wagon, an Indian child's black head disappears into the willow bushes. The skillet lays upside down in the dirt. Charlie stands with a rock in his hand, wailing, "She stole my bacon!"

~ ~ ~ ~

A pre-adolescent Indian child steps into the firelight, hands over head. Thomas follows, his rifle pointed at the youngster's back. Jessie hangs behind, her eyes wide.

Sarah comes forward. "You threatened her with the gun, Thomas?"

"There was no other way." He leans the rifle against the wagon and gestures at the child. "It looks like he's been living on raw duck eggs and berries."

"Poor thing." She looks at the child, then at Thomas. "He?" she asks.

"He's wearing breeches," Thomas points out. "The long hair fooled you."

Sarah crouches in front of the boy and reaches up to gently pull down his left hand. "Hungry?" she asks.

He looks at her stoically. Jessie comes forward with a piece of bread smeared with butter and jam. The boy lowers his right hand and takes it cautiously. Sarah smiles and nods, and he begins to eat.

~ ~ ~ ~

The Pollocks call him John because he came out of the wilderness like John the Baptist. They cut his matted hair and wash his clothes, and he's definitely more civilized, but he's still an Indian. They aren't sure what kind.

When they arrive in Elizabethtown, they find an old trapper who speaks a smattering of Native languages. It takes only a brief interchange with the boy before Old One Eye Pete announces, "He's Navajo. I'm guessin' he's an orphan run away from Fort Union on the Long Walk."

"The Long Walk?" Thomas asks.

"General Carleton had Kit Carson round up the Navajos and put them at Bosque Redondo Reservation to starve." The trapper says. He moves away from the boy. "Now there's talk of sending 'em home."

"But he's an orphan," Sarah protests.

"They're still his people," Thomas tells her.

"How would he get there?"

"Carleton would say that Injuns can always find their way," Old Pete says drily.

~ ~ ~ ~

"And this young man?" the census taker J.B. McCullough asks. He points his pencil at the Indian boy who's just carried in an armload of firewood.

"His name is John," Thomas says. "John Pollock."

"Age?"

"About twelve."

"Birthplace?"

There's a pause. Thomas looks at Sarah, who stands motionless, holding her mixing bowl. "Navajo Indian Country," he says reluctantly.

"Can he speak English? Read and write?"

Thomas turns. "John?"

The boy comes forward. He looks into McCullough's eyes. "Mama Pollock is teaching me," he says.

The man looks at Thomas. "Well, you know what you're doing, I guess." He tucks his pencil into his shirt pocket. "Good luck to you." He nods to Sarah. "Ma'am."

The door closes.

"Bastard," Thomas mutters.

"It's all right," the boy says. "I'm used to it."

Sarah looks at him, her face stricken. "Oh, John," she says. "I'm so sorry."

~ ~ ~ ~

Mama Pollock has explained the Christmas story to John and, though he is skeptical, the Navajo child has enough sense to keep his opinion to himself.

But when Jessie tells him the Christmas legend of the beasts, he isn't quite so polite. He looks up from his slate and the sums Mama Pollock has assigned him. "The animals kneel each year in memory of a baby born long ago?" he asks. "Why would they do that?"

Jessie takes a break from the endless loops of her penmanship practice. "It's because the baby Jesus was God."

"Who told you this story of kneeling animals?"

"Ellen Pascoe. She says her daddy saw it in England when he was a boy."

The Indian child considers this. He likes Ellen Pascoe's dairy farmer father, one of the few Etown citizens who nods politely when they meet. "But this is nuevomexico," he says.

"He says it can happen even here, if we have faith."

John raises an eyebrow, but just then Mama Pollock turns from the fire and asks, "How is the schoolwork going?" and the children return to their slates.

~ ~ ~ ~

Somehow, they manage to slip out of the cabin on Christmas Eve night without waking Jessie's parents. John wonders uneasily whether the adults are really asleep or will be waiting for them when he and Jessie return, but Jessie's hand on his sleeve keeps him going.

Luckily, there's just enough moonlight to make out the frozen ruts in Elizabethtown's streets as they pick their way toward George Clayton's livery stable, where there are sure to be animals.

But as they round the final corner, men's voices spill from the saloon opposite the stable. The children shrink into the shadows.

Two men cross the street, calling, "Clayton! Roust yourself!"

Jessie lets out an exasperated sigh and tugs on John's sleeve. "Come on," she hisses.

"Where to?"

"Mr. Pascoe's dairy."

It will be a long cold walk down the hill to the dairy on the outskirts of town, but in the eighteen months he's known her, John has never heard anyone say "No" to Jessie Pollock. Besides, he likes being outdoors under the stars. He says a silent prayer to Jessie's god that her parents are still asleep and moves forward beside her.

The holiday season has been accompanied by a sudden cold snap, so Henry Pascoe and his Irish assistant have barned the dairy animals instead of leaving them out to pasture. Jessie and John slip through a small side door and stand in the darkness, inhaling the damp, slightly sour aroma as the big white cows shift in their straw.

Once his eyes adjust, John finds a straw bale in the corner and he and Jessie perch on it and peer at the grayish shapes in their stalls.

They sit for only a short while before Jessie whispers, "How long until it's midnight?"

"I can go outside and look at the stars," John offers.

Jessie grips his arm. "Don't leave me. It's dark."

She's such a strange mixture of bravery and fear, he thinks protectively. "All right," he says. "Let's just wait. If the story is true, we'll know when it's time, because they'll all kneel."

"I guess so," she says, staring at the stalls. "It's so dark."

They settle down to wait, shoulders touching, the warmth of the animals and each other drowsing them into sleep no matter how hard they try to keep their heavy eyes open.

Suddenly, there's a great metallic screech. John and Jessie startle awake and look around wildly. It's still full dark, but lantern light flares upward in the ten-foot-high crack between the massive barn doors to their left.

"Well, if ye ain't been caught nappin', I'm a golden-haired fairy king!" an Irish voice says as the light constricts and comes closer. The man chuckles, then the lantern light shifts again as he turns and beckons toward the door. "Ellen girlie, look what I found ye!"

As Ellen Pascoe slips through the door, there's a sudden movement in the stalls. The man and children turn. The big animals are shifting, heads swinging toward the lantern and voices as they begin to lift themselves out of sleep.

"They're bowing," Jessie says, her voice soft with awe.

John opens his mouth to contradict her, to point out that the beasts have been sleeping and were roused by the light. But then Ellen moves forward and the Irishman swings the lantern higher. The two nearest cows are kneeling on their front legs, hind legs extended into the air, sleepy faces dazed by the light.

The girls look at each other, eyes wide, and John finds himself silenced by their desire to believe.

~ ~ ~ ~

It has been what Mama Pollock calls three years since her family rescued John from the wilderness. She stands behind him, studying the columns of numbers on his slate.

"You have a gift for figures, John," Sarah says. She pats his shoulder, returns the slate to him, and reaches across the table for Jessie's work.

"I wish you'd let me sit beside John," Jessie says.

Her mother looks up. "You'd copy his work and wouldn't learn anything."

Jessie and John look at each other and grin.

Charlie comes in the door. "Lesson time, Charles," Sarah says, returning Jessie's slate to her.

"But it's still daylight," Charlie protests. "John's gonna teach me to throw a knife."

Sarah puts her hands on her hips. "Lesson time!" she says sharply. "You need civilizing more than you need to learn how to throw knives." She turns to John. "Please don't encourage him."

~ ~ ~ ~

The Elizabethtown gold mining venture hasn't worked out as well as he'd hoped, and now there's a letter from Ohio, telling Thomas Pollock that his father has died and there's land for him, if he wants to farm it. He stands with the paper in his hand, looking at his wife.

Sarah gazes back at him over the bowl of potatoes she's peeling. "What about John?" she asks.

"What about him?"

"A Navajo boy in Ohio. What kind of life will that be?"

"The mining hasn't amounted to anything much and it's getting poorer," Thomas points out. "We have to eat."

"We can't just leave him."

"There are other boys here on their own."

She lifts her chin. "They wouldn't be, if they were mine."

He grins, knowing this is true. "I don't have to decide right away," he says.

She nods and returns to her potatoes, her eyes troubled.

~ ~ ~ ~

"I need to find my family," John says.

"We are your family," Sarah protests.

The sixteen-year-old shakes his head. "You have been very kind—"

Sarah sinks into her rocking chair. "We tried to make you love us."

"No matter how I feel, I am still Diné," he says gently.

She looks up at him. "Oh, John."

"Jessie will get older, and I will be an obstacle to her suitors."

Sarah waves her hand. "That's a long time coming."

"Not so very long." He moves restlessly. "I don't belong here. Not really." He wonders whether he will belong in Navajo land, now that he's learned the White ways. His habits have changed. Even speaking English has become less of an effort. But she's only done what she thought best and he feels a twinge of guilt as he faces her. "I must go," he says.

She turns her head away.

~ ~ ~ ~

"Well then," Thomas Pollock says, extending his hand.

John grips the older man's palm hard as he shakes it.

"You have what you need?" Thomas asks.

John nods. He looks at the Pollock wagon, loaded for the trek eastward over the Santa Fe Trail, then to Ohio. The three children stand silently beside it. Charlie looks glumly at the ground. Jessie gazes skyward, mouth set tight against angry tears.

Only little Josephine looks him in the eyes. "I wish you would come with us," she says again.

Wordlessly, John shakes his head.

Sarah appears in the doorway of the now-empty cabin. She raises a hand in farewell, lips trying to smile. "God go with you," she says.

"And with you," John answers. He turns abruptly away and begins walking south, toward Palo Flechado Pass and then Taos. He will go westward from there. "Home," he tells himself. But he feels nothing.

~ ~ ~ ~

John Pollock realizes with surprise that he has missed the glare from the red rocks, the harshness of the sun-blasted heat. He stands, feet slightly apart, feeling the stone and sand beneath him, and gazes at the sky and rugged mesas.

Words come back to him, long-buried Diné words praising Creator and creation. He breaths in the hot dry air. It is good to be home.

He begins walking again. Somewhere there will be cousins. Perhaps aunts and uncles. He has the money he earned in the mines as well as the gold Thomas Pollock pressed into his hand as he said, "You take care now," early that final morning.

Perhaps he will buy sheep and drive them to pasture as his grandfather did before the Long Walk. His mind shears off from remembering the Walk itself, that dark and hungry time. And the time in the wilderness after he ran away from Fort Union.

"Somewhere there will be cousins," he tells himself.

~ ~ ~ ~

"You must send them away to school," the Indian Agent says firmly. He gestures toward the four children clustered behind John Pollock and his wife in the dusty Agent's office. "It's the law."

"Not Navajo law," John Pollock says.

"How else are they going to learn to read and write?"

"I will teach them."

"You speak English, but—"

"I also read and write it."

"All adult Navajos are illiterate. Everyone knows that."

John's eyes glint with amusement. "If you say so."

"The soldiers will throw you into prison."

John's wife stiffens, but John smiles gently. "We will see," he says, turning to leave.

"We'll stop your rations."

John opens the office door. "We have mutton and corn." He gestures his family through the doorway and nods politely. "Good day to you. I expect we will not meet again."

"Educated Indians," the Agent mutters as the door closes. "God help me!"

~ ~ ~ ~

At twenty-six, Josephine Pollock is radiant the day she marries the local banker's son in the front parlor of her family's Ohio farmhouse.

In the back parlor, the wedding gifts wait for the guests to admire them. Josephine's older sister Jessie watches over the array.

Josephine's new mother-in-law escorts the groom's great aunt into the room. They pause, considering the bounty.

"What is that thing?" the old lady asks, indicating the large mahogany-colored Navajo pot that gleams from the center of the longest table.

"They tell me it's pottery," the mother-in-law says. "It's from someone the Pollocks knew in Indian Territory, before they came back home."

Jessie, who has been straightening the silver spoons yet again, turns to explain, then thinks better of it. Only those who bother to read the small card beside the pot will ask her who John Pollock is. But no one has yet done so.[26]

---

[26] John Pollock, age 12 and born in Navajo Territory, is the only Native American listed in the 1870 U.S. Census data for Elizabethtown, New Mexico. The Census shows his family members as Ohio-born Thomas Pollock, age 41, gold miner; Sarah Pollock, age 24, also born in Ohio; Jessie F. Pollock, age 8, born in Colorado; Charles L. Pollock, age 5, born in Nebraska; and Josephine Pollock, age 2, born in Colorado. The Census also indicates that John, like the rest of the Pollock family, could read and write. This was unusual for the time. None of the Native Americans in Lucien Maxwell's Cimarron 1870 household were reported to be literate.

This story imagines how this family grouping came about, as well as its fate. The incident in Cimarron canyon is based on the fact that orphaned Navajo children en route to incarceration at Bosque Redondo were detained at Fort Union. Some of those children escaped into the mountains that include Cimarron canyon.

The final story segments are based on the 1880 U.S. Census data, which show that the Pollocks had returned to Ohio by that time, but does not include John in their household.

A Good Christian Girl

By the time she was eleven, Jezebel Goodacre had nine younger sisters and a boundless fury against her father Abraham and her mother Ruth. Every new attempt for a baby boy drew her more tightly into herself and deepened her disgust.

However, no one saw the ferocity of her anger. Like a well-trained child, Jessie kept her brown hair combed and braided, her sky blue eyes on the ground, and her lips sealed. Even when sanctimonious strangers commented on what a full quiver her parents had, or when her mother commented that she'd have plenty of help when a boy did arrive, Jessie remained silent, her bare toe drawing lines in the dusty ground, her hands behind her back as behooved a good Christian girl.

Shortly after Jessie turned twelve, a boy child finally arrived. Abraham and Ruth named him Isaac, and Abraham's interest in his daughters, never strong, became nonexistent. Even Orpah, the golden haired youngest, was ignored for the mewling of the red headed infant.

With the baby's advent, even more of the cooking and housekeeping fell to the three oldest daughters, now twelve, eleven, and almost ten. And when that work was done for the day, they were drafted into the fields: scattering wheat seed behind the harrow, raking into long windrows the hay felled by their father's scythe, hoeing the acreage set aside for potatoes and peas. The work was unceasing, the unending labor broken only by the occasional traveler on his way to anywhere but their mountain valley farm.

Jessie and eleven-year-old Tabitha were breaking new ground for potatoes when the stranger arrived. Tabi's task was to grub out the larger rocks with a thick metal hoe while Jessie followed with the shovel, which was taller than she was. She used the spaces where the rocks had been as starting points, wedging the shovel in as best as she could, then hopping onto its back edge to jam the blade in as far as possible before she lost traction and twisted back onto the ground.

The traveler had reined in his tired-looking brown mule at the edge of the field and watched the girls for several minutes before they looked up and saw him.

He held the reins in one hand and a black book in the other. "Ah, train up a child in the way he shall go and when he is old he will not depart from it," he said approvingly, his long-jawed face nodding at the green plants beyond them. He turned his gaze to the girls, black eyes shiny. "I see that you young ladies are well trained. Surely, your price as women will be far above rubies."

The sisters exchanged glances. "Preacher," Jessie muttered and Tabi nodded, her flax flower blue eyes on the man's face.

"Are you come to sup?" she asked. "Our pa will be most proud to feed you."

"I'll run and tell ma," Jessie said, turning away.

The man watched her go, then looked down at Tabitha. "And how many are you?" he asked.

"There are thirteen of us," the girl said demurely. "Ten girls and a baby boy, besides our ma and our pa."

As Jessie reached the end of the potato field, she heard the man laugh. "Like the prophets of old, they worked until they secured their lineage," he said approvingly.

Jessie scowled angrily, but the expression on her face was carefully neutral by the time she reached the two-rooms-and-a-loft cabin that housed them all. She delivered her message calmly and endured her mother's rush of commands for preparing the house for their guest and ensuring there was enough food in the pot.

Sixth daughter Leah was commandeered to wash the faces and hands of the youngest four and the top-middle girls started a systematic reorganization of scattered dishes, bedding, and petticoats while Jessie pulled out the small barrel of wheat flour to prepare dumplings for the stew that simmered perpetually on the hearth.

Ruth clutched baby Isaac in one arm while she tugged ineffectually with her free hand at the blankets on the marital bed in the corner of the main room. "Jessie, come help me," she ordered. "Those dumplings can wait a minute. He's not reached the house yet."

Jessie put the flour and lard mixture aside and crossed to the bed. Her mother pulled back and looked around the room while Jezebel worked. "Leah!" Ruth said. "Go find your pa and tell him we've got company!"

Leah was crouched in front of Rahab, the second youngest daughter, dabbing at her face with a damp rag. Impatiently, she spit on a finger, wiped a smudge off the toddler's cheek, and stood. "I thought Pa went hunting," she said, looking perplexed. "How'll I find him?"

"Oh, that's right." Ruth paused, considering. "Just go to the edge of that patch of aspen above the second bend in the creek and holler for him. He should hear you from there."

Jessie, now folding blankets at the foot of the bed, looked up and the two girls exchanged glances. Pa was hunting all right. Hunting liquor from his wheat-grain still. But neither spoke it aloud and Leah dropped her rag on the table and slipped out the door just as Tabitha and the preacher reached the dusty cabin yard.

When Leah and her father returned, the preacher was ensconced before the fire in the one Goodacre chair with arms and a seat cushion. Ruth sat on a stool nearby, holding the baby.

Abraham was not obviously tipsy but, from the table in the kitchen area, Jessie could see the brightness in his eyes that said he had indeed been evaluating the market readiness of his still's output.

As Abraham moved forward, the preacher rose and Ruth said, "Husband, this is William Bonecutter, a minister of the Methodist Episcopals." She nodded to the preacher. "My husband, Abraham."

The men shook hands in the middle of the room and the preacher swept his hand at the children scattered around its edges. "You've got yourself quite a quiver full here!" he said. "God has blessed you right mightily!"

"He surely has," Abraham said. He nodded toward the baby. "And He's finally given us a son!" He frowned a little and looked anxiously at the preacher. "I don't know much about the Methodist Episcopals," he said. "Would you see fit to a baptism for the boy? A proper naming ceremony?"

At the table, Jezebel scowled and angrily jammed her mixing spoon into the dumpling batter. There had been no baptism or naming ceremony for Rahab or Orpah. Or any of the other girls, as far as she knew.

"Well, we don't rightly agree with the idea of child baptism," Preacher Bonecutter said. "But a blessing certainly would seem to be in order!" He looked toward the stew pot. "Perhaps after we dine, I can say a few words and then we can pray over the child."

Jessie had been in the potato field early that morning and she was more tired than usual, so the preacher's "few words" after supper seemed to go on forever. She didn't want to listen to him anyway. How dare he support her parent's worship of that baby just because he was a boy and not a girl!

She sat between Leah and Tabitha on the bed in the corner and cuddled Orpah in her lap as if to compensate for the parental neglect, letting the little girl's body warmth drowse her into a half-sleep, the minister's words coming to her disjointedly from where he stood by the fire, long jaw moving steadily.

He said something about "Abraham of old" and "the great patriarchs," then launched into a litany of the blessings we all receive from the all-powerful and omniscient Father God. Food and shelter...clothing and family...dominion over the dumb...the very breath in our nostrils…should be grateful…ready to sacrifice…dearest to us….

Orpah's fist pushed uncomfortably into Jessie's stomach, and the older girl forced her eyes open and rearranged her little sister's limbs as the preacher proclaimed, "When God demands from us a portion of what He has given from His great bounty, it is only right that we offer it back to him gladly, a holy and living sacrifice!"

On Jessie's right, Leah had settled into her own half-asleep state, but Tabi, to Jessie's left, sat straight-backed, leaning forward, her eyes glued to the preacher's face.

Jezebel glanced toward the fire. Her mother was sitting on the stool, head bent, nursing the baby. Her father sat in the good chair. His eyes had lost their brightness, but the alcohol was still evident in the way he clutched the chair arms and leaned toward the preacher, nodding at every third sentence. "Amen!" he muttered as the minister paused for breath. "You speak truth!"

"Even as Abraham sacrificed his own son!" Preacher Bonecutter said. "Now there was a great man, a man who was willing to give up everything for his God. Even his son, the child of his heart, the boy who he'd thought would never arrive." The man's black eyes swept the room, stirring even the sleeping Orpah. Jezebel felt Tabitha shiver with excitement.

"The patriarchs of old were not afraid of great sacrifice!" the preacher continued. "They were willing to give up all that was dear to them because God was dearer to them than all they possessed! And they did it with forethought and enthusiasm! Abraham climbed Mount Moriah eagerly, knowing that God had asked him to sacrifice his child!"

In the chair, Jessie's father leaned further forward, pale blue eyes riveted to the preacher's face.

"That was a long and difficult journey up a mountain far greater than those that surround us in this valley here!" Preacher Bonecutter continued. "Every step that the great patriarch took, he took knowing he would give up his child at the end! But he went! He went valiantly! He went gloriously! He went knowing God's will must triumph over mere man's desire!"

Orpah snuggled her head against Jessie's chest and, despite the preacher's voice and the tension in Tabi's rapt body beside her, Jessie felt herself being curled forward again into the toddler's relaxed state. Only when the preaching finally stopped and her parents rose for the baby's blessing, did her eyes blink open again.

Her father was standing in front of the fire now, a dazed, perplexed look on his face and Isaac in his arms. Her mother stood beside him, adjusting her gown around her swollen breasts.

As Jessie watched sleepily, the preacher took his place in front of them, clutched his black Bible to his chest and intoned, "Oh heavenly Father, we ask that You bless this child as You blessed Isaac long ago, that You give him great flocks and lands, and that You raise him up as a mighty nation that all men will turn to and honor and glorify Your name when they speak of him. We ask that You grant these dear parents the strength to sacrifice all to

You, to honor Your goodness and Your will in all that they do, to be willing to give up even this precious child if You ask it of them." The preacher moved forward and placed a hand on the baby's tiny head. "We ask this in Jesus' name, Amen."

As if on cue, Isaac began to wail. Ruth moved forward, took the child from Abraham's arms, and turned toward the corner. "Jessie, it's late," she said. "Get your sisters to bed, now, like a good girl."

Jessie stirred reluctantly, rearranging Orpah, but Tabi jumped eagerly off the bed. "I'll do it, ma. I ain't tired."

"What a good Christian girl!" the minister said approvingly.

Abraham still looked dazed. He sank back into his chair and gazed at the fire as Ruth directed the sleeping arrangements. Preacher Bonecutter would take Abraham and Ruth's bed in the corner, and she and Abraham would sleep on a pallet in the side room with the younger girls. She stood, holding Isaac and chatting with the minister, as the older girls put the younger ones down and straggled to their own beds in the loft.

The other girls were already asleep by the time Jessie climbed the ladder and pulled on her nightdress. Except for Tabi, who gazed wide-eyed into the firelight-tinged darkness.

Below, their mother asked, "Husband, are you ready for sleep?" and their father mumbled something incoherent. Ruth said, "Well, take the baby then, until he settles," and a few minutes later the door to the side room clicked shut and the preacher began snoring in the corner.

Jessie took a deep breath and settled herself to sleep, but found that she was merely drifting, as half-awake now as she'd been half-asleep before. So when Tabi rose from her blankets an hour later, Jessie was sleepily aware of her sister's movement across the loft and down the ladder. She turned her head, squinting her eyes against the light that still glowed from the fire below, and yawned, wondering where her sister was going.

Her father spoke from the fireside and Tabi's answer was so hissingly intense that Jessie woke completely. She crept to the top of the ladder and leaned forward, straining to hear.

"A true sacrifice," Tabi said. Then she lowered her voice and Jessie couldn't make out her words.

"What God would want," her father said mournfully. "Like Abraham of old."

Jessie leaned carefully out from the side of the loft. She could just see her father's head, Tabi leaning toward him, hissing into his ear. He nodded and shifted out of Jessie's sight, then came into view again, moving toward the kitchen area, the baby in the crook of his arm.

Jessie frowned. He was walking as if he was half-asleep, yet he held the baby firmly enough. He fumbled in the wooden box that contained the kitchen knives and pulled out the largest, the one Ruth and the older girls used for butchering the occasional venison Abraham brought home.

He looked down at it for a long moment, then toward the fire. "Help me!" he whispered, and Tabitha came into view, took the baby from her father, and laid him on the wooden table. As the girl pulled the blankets away from her baby brother's chest and her father raised the knife, Jezebel sucked in her breath.

"No!" she screamed and her father's head snapped toward her, the knife clattering to the floor.

Tabi glared up at her, blue eyes snapping with fury. "It's a sacrifice!" she said, but Jezebel only shook her head wildly and scrambled down the ladder as the door to the side room opened, her mother appeared, and Preacher Bonecutter sat up sleepily and blinked his eyes.[27]

---

[27] This story is completely fictional. Preacher Bonecutter is not based on any of the Protestant missionaries who served in New Mexico Territory.

INDECISION

Billy Dupre pulled his ivory-handled Colt pistol from its holster and laid it beside him on the granite boulder. He looked at the revolver thoughtfully, then twisted away to gaze at the valley below. The morning light was just beginning to turn the tops of the western mountains a pinkish orange. He sighed and shook his head.

"You backin' and fillin' again?" a sleepy voice asked from the other side of the burned out fire.

Billy glanced around. "I can't help it, Johnny," he said. "I just can't get to makin' up my mind to killin' a man just cuz I'm paid to do it. A man who never did nothin' to me or mine. Someone I don't even know."

"You were in the army, same as me," Johnny Kemp said. "You did it then, didn't ya?"

"That was war. This is different."

"And you're from Missouri, same as me," Kemp persisted. "Weren't there no bushwhackers where you come from?"

"Yep, and I shot my share. But that was defendin' my family and my home, same as when I joined up." Billy looked toward the sunlit mountain peaks. "Not that it did me much good. By the time I got back, my ma was dead, my pa was half crazy, and that Sally Ann—" He stood abruptly and nudged at the ashes in the fire ring with his booted toe. "There's no embers left. You got a match?"

"That girl done and gone, didn't she?" Johnny sat up and reached for his knapsack. He pulled out a small canister of matches and tucked it into his shirt pocket. "That Sally Ann?"

"It's all done and gone." Billy turned and began moving around the edge of the campsite, collecting small pieces of downed aspen branches. "All of it's right done and gone."

"So you should be wrathful enough to shoot just about any varmint that crosses your path." Kemp stood, stretched, and began buckling his pants. "Cuz there's no one left back there and no one here neither." He grinned. "No one 'sides me." He crossed to the boulder and hefted the Colt, then flipped it expertly, feeling the balance of the thing. "Nice gun," he said.

"No, you can't have it," Billy said. He dropped an armload of wood beside the fire ring.

Kemp grinned, put the pistol back on the rock, and crossed to the firewood. "So what're you gonna do if you don't go to shootin' for pay?" He crouched down, took out his knife, and began cutting shavings into a small pile. "You gonna go back to laborin' at one of those Etown sawmills? Become a mine flunky?"

"I might." Billy went back to the big rock. He stared down at the valley as he reholstered the pistol. "We had us a farm in Missouri," he said thoughtfully.

Johnny Kemp rocked back on his heels. An incredulous grin split his face. "You gonna be a farmer? A bug ridden, land rich, cash poor dirt grubber?"

Billy Dupre stared at the sunlight touching the grasses below and glinting off the small streams that meandered across the valley toward the canyon of the Cimarron. "I might," he said. "I just might."[28]

---

[28] According to the 1870 U.S. census data, the men in this story were laborers in the Ute Creek/Baldy Mountain precinct east of Elizabethtown. There is no evidence that either of them was interested in or turned to a life of crime. However, since they were both from Missouri and 29 years old in 1870, there's a good chance they'd seen action during the Civil War and/or the bushwhacking that tore Missouri apart before, during, and after that conflict. The Colfax County war that erupted in the early 1870s certainly would have given them opportunity to exercise any gun skills they might have already developed.

NEWS

There was a knothole in the cabin door, in the fourth board from the right. Kenneth stood on tiptoe and peered through it at the men on the horses.

"It's Clay Allison!" he hissed.

His little sister Elizabeth stretched as tall as she could and tried to shoulder Kenneth out the way so she could see for herself. "Are you sure?" she whispered.

Kenneth nodded. "He's tall and he's got those black whiskers and he's ridin' that big blond horse Papa says is so dangerous."

Elizabeth bit her lip and shrank back. She hugged herself tightly around her waist. "I'm scared," she whimpered. "I've heard tell that he's mean."

"Ah, he's only mean to those who are mean," Kenneth scoffed. But he didn't open the door. His mother had instructed him to stay inside if anyone came while she and his father were gone. As far as Kenneth was concerned, 'anyone' included the gunslinger Clay Allison. If that's who it was. He wasn't at all certain, now that he thought about it. He'd never seen the man close up. But he sure wasn't gonna tell Elizabeth that.

The knothole suddenly went black and there was a thud on the wooden door that shook Kenneth in his boots. "What are we going to do?" Elizabeth gasped.

Kenneth put his hand over her mouth. "Hush!" he hissed. "He'll hear ya!"

Boots scuffed on the porch, as if whoever it was had walked away and then come back. "I believe you two young uns ought to open this door," a man's deep voice said. "Your Mama says you won't be wantin' too, but I've got important news for ya'll."

The children looked at each other. Kenneth shook his head.

"But he'll break the door down!" Elizabeth hissed. "And if he has to do that, he'll be really mad! And then he'll be extra mean!"

Kenneth's lower lip jutted out and he shook his head again.

Elizabeth had seen that look before and she knew it was no use arguing with him. She sank to the floor in a heap and tried not to cry.

There was a long silence. Booted feet paced the porch. Then they stopped outside the door again. The man coughed. The children looked at each other apprehensively.

"All right," the man said. "I guess I'll just have to tell you my news through the door. Your Mama's been laid up at your Aunt Ginny's house and she says you're to stay here until your Pa comes for you. That'll more than likely not be 'til tomorrow. She says to have your chores done and your things ready, because your Pa's gonna be taking you back to Ginny's house so's you can meet your new baby brother." There was a short pause. "Or sister. Your Mama doesn't know yet just which it'll be."

The children stared at each other, then Kenneth moved to the door and looked through the knothole again. "Really and truly?" he asked.

"Really and truly," Clay Allison said.[29]

---

[29] Gunslinger Clay Allison claimed he never killed a man who didn't need killing. The Confederate Civil War veteran is responsible for a number of the bullet holes still visible in the tin ceiling of the bar of Cimarron's historic St. James Hotel. However, he is also said to have had a soft spot for women and children.

Obsessions

"Did you know the Maxwell Land Grant Company is evicting people who've been farming here for decades?" the Reverend Franklin Tolby demands.

At the other end of the small pine table, Mary Tolby moves a raised biscuit from the chipped ceramic platter to her plate. "That's terrible," she says. "These biscuits are quite good this time. I think I've finally become used to that stove. Rachel, eat your peas or there'll be no dessert."

Her husband picks absently at his food. "It's a moral outrage," he says. "The Company has no right."

Mary looks anxiously at his pale face. Since they arrived in Cimarron, Franklin has been on horseback constantly, west to Elizabethtown, south to Fort Union and beyond, yet his cheeks show no evidence of windburn or sun.

"I've made strawberry pie for desert," she says. "An Indian girl came by selling berries. They're very sweet. The result should be quite tasty."

Franklin's eyes focus on her for a split second, then his head snaps up, as if he's listening to something outside the house. "And the Indians," he says. "With this much land, there's room for them also." He pauses for a long moment, fork in the air, then says, "Excuse me," drops his frayed linen napkin onto the table, and hurries from the room.

Mary can hear him scrabbling through the papers on his desk as he prepares to write down whatever has just come to him. She sighs and reaches to cover the food on his half-empty plate with a clean napkin. "Rachel, eat your peas," she says absently.

~ ~ ~ ~

The tiny Elizabethtown church reeks with the late June stench of unwashed miners, but Dr. Robert Longwill presses through the door anyway. He nods at Old One Eye Pete, who's standing to one side, his battered hat clasped politely in his hands.

Then the doctor focuses on the front of the room. He can just see the top of Reverend Tolby's head. On Cimarron's dusty streets, the little man's carefully groomed handlebar mustache has often given Longwill the urge to laugh, but here in Etown the miners and old trappers aren't snickering.

Tolby's voice fills the room. "The Maxwell Land Grant Company has no right to the land on which your mines and farmlands rest," he says flatly. "You work the land and bring forth value from it. They sit in their offices and collect the rewards of your God-driven labor. Let us be done with such greed! Let us return to the scriptural truth that a man must work by the sweat of his brow and reap the labor of his hands!"

Dr. Longwill eases out the church door and down the hillside, toward the livery stable where he left his horse. "That preacher's been here less than six months, and already he's an expert on the Grant and the miners' and farmers' rights," he mutters bitterly. Which wouldn't be a problem, if no one were listening to him.

~ ~ ~ ~

Mary Tolby frowns at the potatoes she's peeling, then out the kitchen window at the dusty Cimarron sky. It seems as if a grit-filled wind has blown every day of the eighteen months since she and Franklin arrived here to begin his Methodist Episcopal mission work. Mary sighs, washes her hands, and lifts the towel that shelters her rising bread dough. It's taking longer than usual to double its size.

But then, Franklin is taking longer than usual to return from his Sunday services at Elizabethtown. He's usually back before Tuesday noon, following his meeting with the church board and various other discussions on Monday.

Mary frowns and looks out the window again. There's so much dust in the air, she can hardly see the sun. Franklin's undoubtedly talking with someone in Etown or Ute Park about the Maxwell Land Grant Company and its wholesale eviction of the miners and small farmers who were here before the corporation purchased the grant.

She shakes her head and returns to her work. She very much doubts that her husband is speaking with anyone about the state of their soul. Not that many people in Colfax County seem to care about God or religion. Land and water are all that matter. That and gold. How she longs sometimes for Indiana!

~ ~ ~ ~

Two days before, the man had hovered outside Etown's tiny Protestant church just long enough to confirm that Franklin Tolby was preaching there. He couldn't stay longer than a few minutes. The air sucked out of his lungs at the thought of Tolby's teachings, so contrary to Holy Church. But he'd been there long enough to confirm that the heretic minister will be traveling down canyon this Tuesday morning, as he always does after a Sunday in Elizabethtown.

The man waits now, rifle tucked to his chest, in the shadow of the big ponderosa at the mouth of Clear Creek. How pleasant it will be to stop the minister's preaching.

The men who are paying him to silence Tolby have other reasons for desiring his death, reasons of power and money and land. But the waiting man cares nothing for these things, although the gold they've given him will be useful enough. He can leave the grant now, take his family someplace where americanos have not yet stolen the land from those who know how to do something useful with it, those whose fathers tilled it before them.

He turns his head, listening. Someone is coming. A man singing a raucous heretical hymn. Tolby, most certainly. The minister will stop at Clear Creek as usual, to water his horse and drink from the hollowed-out wooden trough placed there for the refreshment of travelers.

His back will be to the big ponderosa that shields the man with the gun. But there is no dishonor in shooting a heretic in the back. A man who will steal one's very soul if he can, destroy the very fabric of one's Catholic life.

The rider in his clay-brown coat dismounts and the gunman eases into position. He holds his breath as his finger touches the trigger, squeezing so gently and slowly that Tolby drops to the ground before the shooter registers the sound of the bullet's discharge, sees the neat hole it makes in the shabby brown coat.[30]

---

[30] The Reverend Franklin Tolby and his wife Mary arrived in Cimarron in early 1874 as Methodist Episcopal missionaries to the Elizabethtown and Cimarron area. At about the same time, the U.S. Department of the Interior determined that the 1.7 million acres claimed by the Maxwell Land Grant and Railway Company was in fact public land and therefore open to homesteading. The Land Grant Company had been putting down miners' riots and evicting farmers since it bought the Grant in 1870, but the Dept. of Interior decision seems to have escalated tensions to new levels.

Reverend Tolby threw himself into the controversy, even going so far as to resurrect a suggestion made almost a decade before that a portion of the Grant be set aside for the Mouache Ute and Jicarilla Apache bands that had inhabited it before the influx of Americans.

Tolby's pronouncements didn't endear him to the Grant's Board and when he was ambushed in Cimarron Canyon, rumors flew that Board member Dr. Robert Longwill had helped hire the killer. Although several men died as a result of the accusations that flew in the weeks following Tolby's murder, the man who actually did the deed and the motives behind his actions were never definitively identified.

SOURCE LIST

Arnold, Samuel. *Eating Up The Santa Fe Trail*. Niwot: UP of Colorado, 1990.

Bodine, John J. *Taos Pueblo, a walk through time*. Tucson: Rio Nuevo Publishers, 1996.

Bryan, Howard. *Wildest of the Wild West*. Santa Fe: Clear Light Publishers, 1988.

Caffey, David L. *Chasing the Santa Fe Ring*. Albuquerque: UNM Press, 2014.

Cobos, Rúben. *A Dictionary of New Mexico and Southern Colorado Spanish*. Santa Fe: Museum of NM Press, 2003.

Espinosa, Aurelio M. *The Folklore of Spain in the American Southwest*. Norman: U of Oklahoma Press, 1990.

Favour, Alpheus. *Old Bill Williams, Mountain Man*. Norman: U of Oklahoma Press, 1962.

Meketa, Jacqueline Dorgan. *Louis Felsenthal, citizen-soldier of Territorial New Mexico*. Albuquerque: UNM Press, 1982.

Freiberger, Harriet. *Lucien Maxwell, villain or visionary*. Santa Fe: Sunstone Press, 1999.

Horgan, Paul. *Great River, the Rio Grande in North American history*. Middletown: Wesleyan UP, 1984.

Maddox, Michael R. *Porter and Ike Stockton, Colorado and New Mexico Border Outlaws*. Colorado: Maddox, 2014.

Montano, Mary. *Tradiciones Nuevomexicanas, Hispano arts and culture of New Mexico*. Albuquerque: UNM Press, 2001.

Moreno Valley Writers Guild. *Lure, Lore, and Legends of the Moreno Valley.* Angel Fire: Columbine Books, 1997.

Müller-Schwarze, Dietland. *The Beaver, its life and impact.* Ithaca: Cornell U Press, 2011.

Murphy, Lawrence R. *Philmont, a history of New Mexico's Cimarron Country.* Albuquerque: UNM Press, 1972.

Oliva, Leo E. *Fort Union and the Frontier Army in the Southwest.* Santa Fe: National Park Service, 1993.

Rockwell, Wilson. *The Utes, a forgotten people.* Montrose: Western Reflections, 2006.

Russell, Carl P. *Firearms, Traps, and Tools of the Mountain Men.* New York: Skyhorse Publishing, 2010.

Simmons, Marc. *Kit Carson and His Three Wives.* Albuquerque: UNM Press, 2003.

Stanley, F. *The Elizabethtown (New Mexico) Story.* Dumas: Stanley, 1961.

Twitchell, Ralph E. *The Leading Facts of New Mexico History.* Cedar Rapids: The Torch Press, 1911.

1st District Court Transcript, Colfax County, New Mexico Territory, Spring 1869 through Fall 1870.

1868-1870 Colfax County Real Estate Records, Colfax County New Mexico Clerk's Office.

1870 and 1880 U.S. Census records. http://ftp.us-census.org/pub/usgenweb/census/nm/colfax. Accessed Spring 2015 and 2016.

Made in the USA
Las Vegas, NV
22 March 2021